Toussaint's BLUE WATER

Pep Noggle

Then I looked, and there before me was the lamb…

– Revelation 14:1

ISBN: 1453729712
ISBN-13: 9781453729717

LCCN: 2010911225
CreateSpace, North Charleston, SC

Dedication

When God took a rib from Adam, he had Debbie in mind. She is my wife and lifetime friend, and I thank God every day for delivering her to me. I was never a perfect child, nor will I ever be a perfect man, yet knowing this about me, she still holds my hand and says, "I love you." For me, these words are enough; for me, it is all that I ever wanted to hear. Thank you, Debbie, I love you too. This book is for you.

Chapter 1

Nobody believed that God was really coming, unless they lived in Toussaint. The main street of Toussaint followed between the confluence of the eastern flow of the Portage and Toussaint Rivers; it was rightfully named Water Street. Like so many other deep-rooted towns with their primeval inheritance planted firmly in the black soil of the Western Lake Erie Basin, the village of Toussaint was steeped in history and its own country ethnicity. Each town knew itself well, but Toussaint knew itself better. When the village had cause to celebrate, all of Toussaint rejoiced, and when the village mourned, Water Street flowed with its shared tears. Children were not born in Toussaint; they were born to Toussaint. Once a soul was given life, it belonged to everyone who flew the Volunteer colors. The sign on the western edge of the village bore testimony to this fact. In large red letters outlined in green on a pure white background, the sign proclaimed:

Welcome to Toussaint
One Heart – One Mind
Gateway To
The Biggest Week in American Birding
Volunteer Football – State Champs
IN GOD WE TRUST

No dates for the events were given, as none were needed. The sign was not intended to provide an introduction to strangers. It was, without apology, a painted wooden monument to honor that which bound them together—their love of God and their devotion to the Volunteer colors, the Red and Green. It was more than enough, until she arrived.

The cruelest month was upon them. May's capricious winds, so promising of summer, so seasoned with winter's last thoughts, vibrated the metal stripping in the door with a low-pitched hum. She sat alone at the far end of the timeworn bar, studying the solitary cube of ice with her long, slender finger around the wet emptiness of her glass. Around she stirred, browsing the crease of temporal things, along the penumbras that blend night into day. In a place where the living keeps the thoughts of who they would like to be, she had her memories. She kept them all, or as it was on this night, they kept her, fixed to the stool at the bar, fingering the remains of her drink with a longing touch. She withdrew her moist finger from the glass, moved her hand to her open mouth, and with a gentle flick of her tongue, she licked the tip of her wet finger, then swallowed hard.

"Would you like another drink, sweetheart?" asked Violet Love as she reached for the empty glass.

"Please," she moaned, a whispered reply, handing the dripping shell to the older, but still beautiful, woman behind the bar.

"Some more blood of an angel, or would you like something with a quieter voice?"

"Is that what you call this potent spirit? The blood of an angel makes me shiver. I would rather be kissed by the Green Fairy." The visitor's voice shuddered with an uncommon lilt as she mimicked a fearful tremble.

"Green Fairy," Violet mused as she rinsed the glass beneath the fresh tap water and then placed it back on the bar top, "that one escapes me."

The guest pointed her perfectly manicured finger at the green solution steeping quietly next to the half-drained bottle of bourbon. "She's winking at you from above, tempting but unattended."

Violet lifted the bottle from the shelf with her left hand. "Are you pointing at this little baby? Nobody ever asked before. It was a gift from my liquor man. It adds to the color of the place. I don't even have a price on it." She caressed the bottle, slowly running her right fingertips over its unfamiliar curves. "Do you know what it's called?"

"Most call it absinthe, while those who know it best call it the Green Fairy. It gathers its properties from the Holy Trinity of wormwood, anise, and fennel. It was once blamed for turning man into beast, transforming the artists and poets who favored her taste. But I know from experience, and so do you, that a man can be a brute without the influence of a spirit."

Violet examined the bottle, turning it carefully to capture its full measure in the light. "It looks harmless enough. Do you want it straight or on the rocks?"

The young beauty reached her right hand across the bar, touching lightly against the supple flesh of Violet's arm. She leaned in close enough for Violet to feel the moist content of her perfumed breath as she spoke.

"There is a tradition to sampling this drink. Would you like to learn?"

Violet smiled and then took in a slow, lingering breath. "I like history."

"Then you will love this. The tradition is to pour whatever amount you desire into a glass. Then, hold a cube of sugar on a spoon over the drink and gently effuse a stream of water over the sugar until the louche is to your liking."

"The louche?"

"Yes, the louche is a milky white cloud that joins men to their dreams."

"Only men?"

"Women too, if they are so inclined."

"Well, how much louche do you like?" Violet lowered the bottle to the top of the bar.

"It depends on your taste for absinthe."

"Well, what is your taste for absinthe?" Violet was drawn in by the details of her strange knowledge and extraordinary looks.

"Forget tradition. My taste is straight, with just enough ice to cool my tongue."

"No louche?"

The beauty ran both of her hands through the silken strands of her raven mane before answering, "No louche!"

Violet opened the bottle with the same reverent manner that she would bestow upon Kentucky bourbon aged twenty years in a charcoal barrel. She dropped two cubes of ice into her glass, which rang familiar to a serious drinker, then poured a rush of green solute as generous as her soul.

"Mother is everything in this life," the young woman pronounced. "She is consolation in time of sorrowing, and hope in the time of grieving, and power in the moments of weakness."

Violet pulled a towel from her snug rear pocket, then wiped the bar top dry. "You are quoting Gibran?"

"You know Gibran, but you don't know about the Green Fairy?"

Violet lifted the bottle to her mouth and took a long tug of the high-octane proof. She did not flinch as the drink crawled into her system with a satisfying burn. "Now I do."

The visitor took a small taste from her glass. "Not yet, but you will soon be touched by her stinging hair."

"Ooooo, sounds ominous," Violet teased.

"It is the truth." The visitor swirled the drink in her glass before placing it back on the bar top.

"The truth?" Violet laughed before downing another mouthful of the licorice-tasting spirit. "The truth will set us free, right?"

The newcomer sighed as she lowered her head over the rim of her glass. "That's what they say. Set yourself free. Tell me the truth about Toussaint."

Violet capped the bottle of absinthe and placed it back upon the shelf. She had an itch to reveal every Toussaint secret to this woman, but she was disciplined with her words. Nothing could impair her judgment about such things. Certainly, two generous swallows of the Green Fairy would not be enough to compel Violet to scratch from within a mind-blabbing cloud of booze to a stranger. She was better than that. She was a premium Toussaint woman. She would only tell what was known to all and what all would be glad to tell if asked.

"The men of Toussaint love God and his three gifts to Toussaint men."

"What three gifts?"

"They love Toussaint women, Toussaint football, and the fertile wetness of Toussaint itself."

"That covers a lot of ground."

"You bet. God can be that way."

"And what do the women of Toussaint love?"

"Toussaint women love Toussaint men."

"And do Toussaint women love God?"

Violet paused before answering. She wiped her palms dry against her tight-denim-covered thighs while the visitor inhaled the vapors of her drink. Then, true to her stewardship of all questions raised at the bar, she delivered.

"You can count on it, darling, and he sends you his love."

"Then we will thank God," the young beauty cried out as she raised her glass to the house. "Yes, we will thank God for all that is, for the loving and the hating, for the giving and the taking; I salute the Almighty for making the rules." She wet her lips with her pink tongue, tilted her head backward as if being kissed on the neck, and then emptied her glass in three soft swallows. "And Violet"—she winked while savoring the taste—"tell God that I love him too."

With nothing more to say, she placed her empty glass on the bar top and unraveled herself from the stool. Every person in the room watched her barelegged exit across the wooden floor. As she opened the door into the night, the damp wind blew a moist puff of her presence throughout the room. Every man caught her scent, and every woman who was with a man ordered one more round to dry his memory.

There was no woman to compare her to in Toussaint, Ohio. She was what a man could only visit in the deepest sleep that shuts out the world. She was a nonpareil, a splendid anomaly without sensual peer. Within moments of her leaving, they could not remember the exact details of her extraordinary appearance; yet, they could not forget that she had been there. She lingered in their senses, like the fragrant air of their rarest fantasy, where details are written on a dream. Her presence on this night provoked the unreal flowing of time, when a single moment shares the characteristics of past, present, and future, and the collective mind is on the same page of the experience.

Working her fingers into the grip, she lifted the scissor-opening door of her black Diablo Roadster and eased behind the wheel. The car, like the woman, was built on lines that Toussaint men could never touch. It was a man's longing for motion and material molded into a smooth, blood-rushing form that remained eternally out of reach. Under her hand the powerful engine inhaled the cool night air and thundered to life. She wheeled away from the curb and headed north, speeding toward Twin Bridges in a haze of willful intent.

The black Diablo roared down the highway without conscience or malice. It was just a car that was being driven by the will of a beautiful woman in a hurry, and as such, the car's response to the changing conditions of the weather and the road could be no more than the driver's skill to recognize and adjust. By the time the wheels broke traction across the slickened surface of the first bridge, the ethereal beauty had already relinquished her ability to recover. Nothing could be done to correct the ease with which the car lifted off the road. Nobody could avoid the inescapable fate of all that was coming their way.

The Diablo was airborne and sailing, ten feet off the ground over the first bridge. It came down between the two bridges, striking the road in a horrific display of metal sparks, shattered glass, and squealing rubber. Amidst the splintering and crumbling of life and machine, the car once more lifted into the air, smashed against the railing before the second bridge, then rolled itself into a molten ball of flaming steel that plunged, sizzling, into the chilled waters of the Toussaint River. As the wreck cooled in the river's embrace, a vapor rose around it that was thicker than fog, but lighter than smoke. It covered the surface of the water in a mist that no eye could penetrate, like a shroud that was sent to cover the horrible aftermath.

The driver saw nothing of what was taking place. Except for the whirling sensation of uncontrollable motion, she felt nothing but the air-swallowing choke of cold water as it rushed into her lungs. As life seeped away from her, she had no power to prevent its leaving. Her last breath was a bitter mixture of river and air that tasted like her past.

Chief Joe "Blue" Water swung slowly off of Route Two. Heading south on Route Nineteen, his police cruiser turned a smooth, deliberate arc beneath his expert touch. The road was a blowing froth of lake water as the western basin breached the shores that contained it. He turned on his wiper blades to remove the hailing rain. The nor'easter was thundering into the warm southwesterlies on Joe's turf. The resulting supercell would guarantee a long night of emergency calls. Hunkering down for the challenge, his radar unit registered a 166-mile-per-hour blur heading his way. He switched on his red, white, and blue flashing lights, reached for his radio, and prepared to call in a pursuit when he witnessed the oncoming headlights rise into the air, fall back to the ground, then explode into a fireball that disappeared into the black water of the river. He pushed the button on the microphone and calmly went to work.

"Dispatcher, this is Water. I have a code four, one-vehicle accident at Twin Bridges. Call everyone to the scene." He paused and took a slow, deep breath. "I'm going to need everyone. The vehicle is in the river. Do you copy this?"

"Yes, Chief," the dispatcher replied. "You have a code four, all call, on Route Nineteen at Twin Bridges; the dispatch time is twenty-three eleven."

"Roger that." Water hung up as he rolled his cruiser to a stop. The chief trained his spotlight on a fixed position in the mist-imbued river while popping the trunk latch and opening the car door in fluid cadence. Joe Water was a man of no wasted motion. He was cool and deliberate in all situations, and a fearless improviser without doubt in his abilities. He slid out of his vehicle, considered the short end of time in the cold and turbid water, and like the river itself, flowed toward his destiny.

He stepped to the back of the cruiser while peeling down to his skivvies and placed the bundle neatly on the floor of the trunk before retrieving a retractable lifeline, a rescue harness, swim fins, goggles, and a diver's headlamp. He clipped a lifeline reel in place on the harness, let out some slack, and then snapped the free end to a steel D-Ring that was shackled to the bumper. Fitting into the harness, fins, goggles, and headlamp, he switched on the light and then opened the bale in order to free the rope. Throughout each efficient step, his focus remained on point in the vapor where he was certain that the submerged car was located. The tranquil and steely Toussaint chief of police was fully prepared to commence his mission. Detached from the howling elements of wind and rain that were bearing down on him, he climbed over the bridge railing and, with outstretched arms and hurdler's legs, splashed feetfirst into the river, making a trained rescue dive entrance.

The immediate shock of icy immersion caused his body to heave and gasp. The pounding in his chest and the ringing in his ears was deafening as his blood left his extremities for the warmer refuge of his body's core. With his head bobbing above the water's surface, he breathed in staccato puffs of wind to quell the violent changes of physical extremes. As the froth of volatile air warmed within his lungs, he quickly regained command of his tremulous, twitching limbs. With sincerity of purpose and willful flesh tamed, he was settled and ready to proceed. Joe Water had been on the scene for just under a minute when he began his swim through the bubbling moil.

The current was swift and mean, but his skills were evenly matched. He swam with powerful, sweeping strokes that he had mastered when his days were longer and nights were protected on his mother's watch. As a boy off the shore of the lake, when the water was kinder and warmer, he learned to streamline his body and pull through the waves with a deep kick and hourglass stroke. Kicking and churning in this lathered-up chop, the lessons learned were tested and true. Stroke by resolute stroke, he cut through the blow with the dogged belief that all things were possible to a man who tried.

The nor'easter's brutal exhaust coughed up an eerie, amber-gilded cloud that swirled through his cupped hands as he closed in on his mark. Swallowing a lungful of the yellow sky, he plunged himself below its cover, searching the black depths for what the Toussaint might reveal.

"Attention all local, county, and state units," the dispatcher's clear voice summoned over the airwaves, "this is Toussaint Dispatcher Debbie Marshall. I have a code four, all call, on State Route Nineteen at Twin Bridges. I repeat…code four, all call, on State Route Nineteen at Twin Bridges. A vehicle is in the river. I repeat…A vehicle is in the river. Chief Water is on the scene."

"This is State Patrol Unit One responding to the all call." The familiar voice was the first to answer.

"I copy that, Unit One."

"County Squad Thirteen responding!"

"I copy that, Thirteen." Dispatcher Marshall acknowledged all incoming calls with the same professional response.

"County Water Rescue leaving the station!"

"I copy that, Water Rescue Team."

As the calls poured into the dispatcher, the police scanner behind Violet Love's bar commanded sobering attention. The tall man shouted to no one in particular. "Let's go! Blue's on the scene waitin' for nobody but the devil! Move it, before he meets poor Scratch and chokes the life out of him!"

The clock was turning, time was pushing against them, and all but one Volunteer was certain to the bone that Blue Water could handle whatever called him into the river.

"Oh my God, no!" Violet cried out as she led the galvanized crowd into the fuming sting of the feral winds.

The tall man slammed his bottle of beer hard upon the bar top and then followed on their heels. Within seconds, Violet's Friendly Tavern emptied, and Route Nineteen was aglow with red-lighted pickup trucks flashing northbound in the crushing hail. The Toussaint Volunteers were on their way, and no unnatural force could stop them, not even the wicked gales spawned from the fickle womb of May.

Joe Water found nothing on his first dive to the muck-imbued bottom. He surfaced, gulped another mouthful of jaundiced gas, and then descended once more. He didn't notice the terrible bluster that was brewing all around him, nor the brackish taste of the air as it wheeled within his body. While the Canadian winds coughed chunks of northern ice into the black backwater of Lake Erie, Joe remained faithful to his duty. With less than two feet of visibility in the rocking flow of silt and debris, he continued to feel around for signs of life. In the haunts of the channel cat and bullhead, Blue Water was just another smooth-skinned hunter.

"Violet, this is Coyote!" the tall man shouted across the open channel. "Pick up, girl! Do you read me?"

Violet tightened her grip on the steering wheel as horizontal sheets of rain and hail poured across her windshield.

"Violet…dagnabbit, girl!" Coyote continued shouting into his microphone. "If you don't ease up, we'll be tendin' to you before we get to Blue. Do you copy that?"

"I copy that!" she cried into her radio. "I copy that…I copy that…" Her voice trailed off the air.

"Then trim your spurs, sweetheart, and maybe we can all live long enough to tell this story over a cold one," Coyote appealed fervently while backing off of the accelerator.

The radios were silent. Apart from the static drone of dead air, nothing occupied the space that was reserved for Violet's response. The convoy of trucks slowed down. The anxiety within each cab was supercharged with the kind of distress that bubbles within a hanging man's gut just before the floor drops away. It was more than darkness and storm and Violet's will that forced the bile up into their troubled throats. In the distance, the crossing gates for the dual set of railroad tracks descended menacingly across the road. With bells blaring in the mix of all that surrounded this place, the flashing twin lights winked a red-eyed warning. The midnight eastbound freight was usually clockwork tight, but tonight it was early. With great bursts of crosswind rolling the train from side to side on rain-slicked rails, Coyote knew better than to challenge for the crossing; so did everyone else, except for Violet.

"Doggone it, Violet!" He broke the silence while pumping the brake.

Hell-bound or heaven-sent, Violet ignored all but her heart as she barreled straight ahead. With its ominous multipitched horn and white-lighted head dividing the night, the eastbound leviathan shook the earth beneath its wheels, causing men and machines to vibrate. The ground moved, the train roared, the rain broke in strobe-lighted effect as headlights converged on the crossing. Coyote blinked, and Violet was gone. The fuming engine thundered past the line of stopped pickups, spewing scraps of the shattered gates into the air. Standing a few feet before the crossing, the yellow sign declared: Don't Blink – Speed Kills! As the sign's image burned into his mind, the remains of the wooden gates reported their splintered condition against his truck. Coyote cupped his large hands over his ears to mute the ghastly scene. Years of volunteering had not prepared him for this. There was nothing in his life that could equal this night, nothing at all…

Joe Water was still holding on to his second breath of air when his right hand struck forcefully against the twisted wreckage. He moved his head to within inches of the disfigured heap to allow the light to penetrate the dreadful environment. The thickened, muddy water forced him to rely on his sense of touch to determine shape from shadow. His headlamp and goggles were of little use on the organic bottom of this stirred-up brew. The best that he could do was to reach and feel, reach and feel, and work his way around the wreck until he found an opening. Reach and feel, reach and feel, find an opening, Joe was running out of air, but he was determined not to surface. Reach and feel, reach and feel, find an opening, but there was none to discover. Whatever shape the wreck had rolled itself into, it did not save room for anyone to enter, or for that matter, to leave.

Joe was becoming cyanotic, yet he remained on the bottom with his mission. *One more reach,* he was thinking, *one more touch. I'm not quitting until I know. Just one more, one more, one more...*

Then suddenly his hand groped the unmistakable firmness of human flesh. It was a human head, attached to a human body, upside down on the river's bottom. Straining to focus his light into the opening, he reached both of his arms into the jagged gap and found the body of a perfectly formed woman, still strapped behind the wheel. While the vehicle was smashed beyond recognition, its driver was situated neatly in a secure space that seemed unaffected by the collision.

I can save her, he thought. *Vagal inhibition, instantaneous death, I can save her.* He was as certain of this as he could be, considering the chemical confusion in his blood.

Exhausting the last bubble of oxygen from his painfully depleted lungs, he reeled a length of slack from his lifeline, tied it securely to the undamaged steering wheel, and then kicked to the top with his body screaming for air. Joe broke the surface, exhaling an explosive load of carbon dioxide into the electrically charged atmosphere. As hail and piercing rain pelted the top of his head, he gulped the bone-chilling boreal air like a spent hound and then panted calmly, replacing the noxious gas with life-giving oxygen. While the storm's carnage circled around the heaving surface about his head, the Toussaint chief calmly scanned the perimeter for rescue assistance. All that he saw was his own line of taut rope rise out of the water and then disappear in a straight line into the amber-blushed mist. He had never experienced such a milieu. There were no Volunteers, a raging wind, and a stationary yellow fog. These conditions were new to him, especially the yellow fog. He had never experienced a yellow fog at all.

State Patrol Unit One was in full cruise through the Magee Marshland with Lieutenant Nathan Swift at the wheel. Swift had more than duty to fulfill on this run. He and Joe Water were friends of a different breed, bound by an unspoken trust since childhood. Their spirits were sewn together with an invisible thread that pulled tighter through the years, years that Toussaint would not put to rest. Every football season since the championship year, the editor of the local paper published an inspirational story in the *High School Preview* of the days when "Swift-Water" poured over Toussaint foes. Joe's nickname could have been a tribute to the pounding that he gave out on Friday nights. Would-be tacklers often came up on the hurtful end of his driving knees and powerful forearms. Bruised and bloodied body parts were delivered randomly to anyone who was predisposed to interfering with his forward progress. He could have been called "Blue" from the violet hue of the contusions left on his victims, but more likely the name came from the blustery blue eye that radiated discordantly aside the dark calm of his brown right eye. When he was at peace, his brown eye commanded your attention, but when he reached the end of his rope, he was all blue-eyed serious. Nathan Swift did not need a nickname; his family name said it all. Faster than any Toussaint boy before or since, Swift was more a right of birth than a name to be considered.

They could have done anything with their lives, but they chose to give themselves to Toussaint. After graduation they took jobs laying the concrete roads that entered the village with square curbs and level surfaces. They had no desire to take the crooked county roads out of town that connected to the interstate and things that were not worth knowing. They already knew who they were and what they wanted to become. When they were ready, they took up the badge, on the same day, at the same hour, to preserve the things that they had known. They did it together, as only men who understand such things can do. Men who know their duty and know it well and serve without regret. They were the best play drawn out of the Volunteer playbook: Swift to the outside of Toussaint as a state trooper and Water to the inside as the chief officer of the peace. There was nothing tricky about it. It was just good football applied to life.

Nate's blood was pouring heavily into his chest as he sped through the richly variegated marshland of the Toussaint. He loved this outer edge of Ottawa County, the remaining wild land of the Great Black Swamp, an area of emerging marsh, wet prairie, and forest beach ridge that once stretched one hundred twenty miles long and forty miles wide across eighteen Ohio counties. The swamp teemed with the exotic and the common forms of the Creator's bounty and was revered by Native Americans as the place where the endless sky crossed the open water. Swift could claim blood ties to the great Shooting Star, the fierce Shawnee chief who was better known to white men as Tecumseh. The fine black hairs on his neck were dancing with the unnatural presence that this place always held for him. He could feel things in the Toussaint that an ordinary man could not. He was feeling that things were not going well for the man whom he called brother.

County Squad Thirteen was now waiting alongside the line of Volunteers at the railroad crossing. The Water Rescue Unit, three fire trucks, a Toussaint police cruiser, and a county sheriff's car soon joined the lineup of stalled rescuers. Prolonging this nightmarish paradox of outcomes, the engineer aboard the eastbound was now attempting to bring the train to a stop in order to survey the damage. This terrible twisting of lives and circumstances was killing the most critical element of salvation: the time to do the job. They could never regain it by any amount of swearing upon deaf ears. It just couldn't get any worse. Nobody's luck was this bad. Every soul in the lineup was being touched by a tempest that had no reason for being except to deliver misery and pain. This night was independent of other natural forces, and if they didn't know it in their thinking, they could feel it crawling across their skin.

Violet Love was still rolling north on Route Nineteen, while Nathan Swift was beginning to make his turn onto Route Nineteen South. Combing the darkness, caught in the ebb and sway of the rush of their lives, they were praying to bend time on this night.

As he took his final deep breath, Joe could hear the sirens in the distance. He knew that he wouldn't be alone much longer. Suddenly, a blinding bolt of light split the night, which gave the appearance of a door opening up on the sun. A tremendous surge of violent energy lifted Joe and heaved him out of the water. His strongest sensation was of burning hair and searing flesh as he soared four stories skyward within the brilliant white flash. As his body hung briefly in midair, he observed a perfect hole in the mist below, his flaming skin, and without fear or pain, an abrupt sense of falling. Joe Water tumbled back through the hole and watched it close in around him with a booming clap. With no ability to control the dynamics of his descent, he smacked the river's surface on his back with a sizzling thud that stopped the mortal rhythm of his good and stalwart heart. Freak lightning on a freak night. With the lifeline burned away from his body, Peace Officer Joe bobbed in the curling waves and then soundlessly settled beneath the cloudy foam that claimed him. Drifting with the nor'easter flotsam and Lake Erie jetsam, he was washed clean of his earthly stain.

Chapter 2

Nathan Swift kept a close ear on his radio and both eyes down the road. He was aware of everything both near and far on this run, and like his lifelong friend, he was predisposed to making something happen. His instincts were forged in the same furnace, tempered by the same extremes, and trued by the same knowledge of life and death that drove them both to this unchanged point in their lives, to serve and protect. Closing in on the scene, he quickly absorbed the details: Joe's lights flashing in the pudding-thick darkness, Violet's headlights growing brighter on the horizon, uprooted trees and marshland vegetation littering the road with their torn remains, and an unseasonable roiling condition of sky and water. It was, to be sure, a bizarre set of circumstances, but it did not slow him down. Less than a mile from Twin Bridges, even the sudden bolt of sonic light that rocked and rattled the earth did not discourage his single-mindedness. Nathan Swift was much like Joe Water in the ways that keep such men alive; except on this night, Nate was still breathing.

"State Patrol Unit One arriving on the scene of the all call…over." His distinctive voice resonated through the radio.

"You're logged in, Lieutenant. The time is twenty-three sixteen." Dispatcher Marshall's voice was firm and precise, professionally cleaned of excess expressions.

"Unit One…clear." Swift's on-air language was much the same.

He pulled his black patrol car alongside Water's white cruiser, blocking both lanes of the rural highway. Side by side, awash in the burn of their emergency lights, the two contrasting vehicles presented an arresting force, just like the men who drove them.

"Here we go again, brother," he said out loud as he aimed his spotlight into the swirling mist, confident that he would find his friend swimming near the bridges. Seeing nothing but Joe's taut lifeline tracing a clean tack into the water, he jumped from his vehicle, grabbed a firm hold on the line, and gave the familiar tug that Joe would recognize on the other end. Immediately he realized that the rope was too tight, too secure, not answering his call.

"Blue!" he hollered into the night. "Blue, where are you, Blood?" He gave another jerk on the line and found the same dead response. In less time than it takes for a man's spit to hit the ground, Nate was stripped down to a prayer and was swimming the crawl with the yellow fog twisting around his head.

"Jesus, Jesus, Jesus!" he bellowed into the fierce wind. "Jesus, it's cold. Jesus, Jesus, Jesus, warm me. Come on, Lord, give me a break." He prayed fervently, trying to gain control of his body with his faith.

"Jesus, you are my light and my salvation, whom shall I fear!" He coughed out the words to his favorite psalm. "Jesus, you are the stronghold of my life, of whom shall I be afraid?" he pled to the one whose crucified image hung on a gold chain around his neck. "Wait for the Lord. Wait for the Lord. I'm coming, Blue! Hold on, Blood! Jesus, it's cold!" Kicking and pulling, kicking and pulling, sinews tightening, ears ringing, past images feeding an emotional chill that was new and unwanted, he reached the visible end of the rope, wolfed in a chestful of hope and whirling air, then dove beneath the surface.

Nate had no light to cut the darkness and no goggles to protect his eyes from the turbulent mix that was surging against him. What he did have in the spooky depths of this eerie backward-flowing river was a perfect blend of man and animal, a symmetry of instinct and intellect that joined his faith in a potent exhibition of confident behavior, as long as the Lord was with him. On his first touch, he found the climber's knot tied to its fixed position, and then he reached up and grabbed the loose end.

Joe is untied! The thought charged through him. The image of his friend in danger caused his stomach to heave. He reached into the open spaces of the water and found nothing. He dug his arms deeply into the black abyss and found no one, not his friend, not a victim, no one. His instinct sensed that Joe had made a rescue, but he reinforced it with a prayer.

Jesus, let Joe be the man on this day! His Christian soul prayed as a fresh salvo of frozen white plague pitched hard against the surface above him. *Jesus, let Joe be on top! Jesus is Lord! Jesus is Lord! Jesus is Lord!* His Christian mantra took on the rhythm of his Indian blood. Nathan Swift held tightly to the rope but tighter to his faith as he followed the angled line back up to the surface.

The squall was now in full force. Assaulted by a malevolent wind that spun around his head in a skin-peeling vortex, kicked and pounded by cattails and swamp grass and airborne soil that raked through his scalp and peppered his eyes with a blinding sting, Nate's own fierce nature gave no quarter. Every particle of this place that he loved had turned against him in a bitter, wind-fired rage. The air imploded as the pressure bottomed out, viciously sucking at his bulging eyeballs, squeezing the tears out in painful blinks of uncertainty, yet he did not submit to this panorama of terror.

"Jesus, what is going on?" he shouted, expecting a divine intervention. "Where are you, Blue? Where are you, Blood?" But nobody answered.

"Joe...Joey!" the voice on the bridge cried out. It was a woman's voice, the voice of panic over unfulfilled dreams. "Joe...Joey!" It was the weeping call of Violet Love.

"Joe...Joey!"

"Blue...Buddy...Blood!"

The two voices found each other above the demented howl of the wind. Violet directed her flashlight toward Nate, who was holding fast to the rope above the wreckage.

"Nate...Nathan Swift!" she screamed, her voice cracking under the strain. "What did you find?"

"Blue's in here somewhere. Check the backwater!"

"What?"

"Check the backwater!"

Obeying his command, Violet turned her attention to the other side of the bridge while Nate used Joe's lifeline to pull himself back to land. Scrambling along the sharpened edges of the limestone shoreline, he compelled his frozen body to respond, knowing that prayers worked better for those who worked harder. The blood-slicked trail that followed behind him was evidence that his prayers and his labors were more than words.

"Jesus is Lord, by God!" He stomped his feet into the organic muck as he made his way toward Violet.

As the last eastbound freight car cleared the crossing, the storm continued to wail against their vehicles. Picking and chewing the paint from their rolling Detroit metal, the whip-tailed elements scourged the convoy, but it did not slow them down. Coyote and his rescuers shot over the tracks, speeding through the oppressive gale, mindful of the fact that time lost could never be regained.

Debbie Marshall sat dutifully at her post with her right hand on the microphone, waiting for the next call. She kept one eye on the clock and the other on the mug of black coffee that was just a short reach from her left hand. She wanted to take a drink, but she was in the zone, doing her job, mobilizing the forces while recording the movements of time. It was twenty-three twenty-nine. Thirteen minutes had passed since Unit One logged in at the scene. She had to stay focused on the running clock. The coffee was probably cold, anyway.

And so it was, with all hands struggling desperately to reach the side of Blue Water, that Joe's body came to rest among the cattails and sedges around the river's bend; lifeless and cold it rose and fell, undulating in the waves. His cyanic skin, macerated and burned, gave forth the pungent smell of violent death. And so it was, in this stirred-up state of nature and man, beyond these circumstances of a sure and certain passing, that his dead body began to breathe.

Joe Water was alive. Even with the glacial rage of the heavens battering the earth around him, he felt peaceful and warm. He had no immediate memory of what had taken place, but he could smell the pureness of his scented past. The remembered aromas of wet grass and spring rain excited his senses, and the breath inside him tasted like he had swallowed life from a perfumed cup. His eyes were closed, but it seemed that he could see through his eyelids, taking in a harmonic flow of colors that melded without and within him. The wind that whistled over and around his still body issued a chorus of melodic sounds that were mellow and pleasing. His whole being felt comfortable in the presence of all that he perceived. Then, in a no less pleasurable or soothing manner, Joe regained consciousness. He opened his eyes to the blackness of the gale, sat up in the shallows, and looked around.

The nor'easter had manifested its full malignancy in its collision with the warm spring air of Ohio. In this aerial maelstrom, this violent whirlpool of unearthly extremes, Joe Water beheld the body of a woman floating faceup beside him. He rose to his knees and then lowered his head over her face, checking her breathing in a way that looked like a lover's embrace. Her beauty was bewitching.

Even in the dire conditions of mud and mire, she was unblemished, sweetly fragrant, warm, and alive. He stood up to his full height, then bent down and lifted her into his arms. He pressed her beautiful head into his chest to protect her from the ravaging wind and then pushed against its blowing mass toward the carnival of lights that gamboled upon the bridges. The rescuers had finally arrived. Toussaint was waiting.

"Joe, my God, Blue...Buddy...Jesus...God... Jesus, thank you...Joe!" Nathan Swift, battered and bloody, rambled on as he ran to meet Joe coming out of the night. "You're the man, Blue! My God, you're the man! Praise Jesus! Jesus is Lord!" His words tolled brightly above the wind and the rain.

Violet Love followed quickly behind Nate. When she saw how tenderly Joe was carrying the young woman from the bar, she stopped, wrapped her arms around her own cold body, and watched silently as the rescuers crowded around their champion. On this night of unfathomable limits, this shortened hour of death and resurrection, Toussaint welcomed back its hero. In this there was no mistake, and during all of the raving and glorified backslapping as the storm twisted itself out over the lake, Joe smiled and said that he was just doing his job. As the Volunteers tended to the wounded, he thanked everyone for answering the call.

When the praise and business end of the night was over and the crowd rolled back to the village, Joe Water would still be on the scene. Standing alone on Twin Bridges, with the ruptured air still crackling around him, he would not leave until his duty was complete. This is the way that things had always been. It was what he liked about his job. Immersed in his purpose, this is the way that it could always be, as long as he remained focused, kept a grip, and stayed the course.

Chapter 3

There are days for every man when he feels invincible. There are days when he is completely free of fear and doubt, and he can honestly carry himself as though he were the greatest man alive. These days are short-lived and greatly wasted during a few precious moments of each man's youth. They come like brilliant flashes of light, and then disappear into the different shades of dark that a man lives in for the remainder of his days. Joe Water was unlike this colorless mixture of monotonous men. His light never faded to gray. He still lived unafraid, being who he had always been during his greatest hours.

The crash was now legend. It was the night of extremes, the time of miracles. The magnitude of the unbelievable had been distilled down to a few observable details that could never be disputed by any other point of reason. The simple truth of what was seen by all who witnessed was that Joe Water walked out of the flooded marshland with the heavenly stranger in his arms. During the hour of the terrible storm, with the mangled remains of her car scattered on the roadway and entombed on the river bottom, all prayers were heard and answered on this night for the Toussaint faithful. No one could challenge this; no one tried. Life could only get better.

The day was breaking bright and clear. It was one of those crack-aired, frosty Lake Erie mornings that wrapped each spoken word in a white, vaporous cloud. Except for the littered aftermath of the superstorm, the marshland was tranquil and golden in the rise and shine of the sun. It would have been a good day for spotting bald eagles or the neotropical migratory birds that winged their way through the Lake Erie flyway between North and South America, but there was work to do. The state patrol had been manning a detour around the site of the accident since the early morning hours. They had established roadblocks at the north and south ends of Route Nineteen to assist the Toussaint Police Department, who had jurisdiction over everything in between. The accident was fully documented, and no charges would be filed, as the chief determined that none were warranted. Written down in Joe's own handwriting, his decision was clearly noted:

The driver was found to be lucid and calm with no evidence of alcohol or drugs. Road conditions were hazardous, causing the driver to lose control over the icy surface. The situation was unavoidable; it was an accident.

This was the whole story that would be entered into the record, and as far as Joe could remember, it represented the truth.

Joe Water cast a long shadow over Twin Bridges as the sunlight radiated across the eastern sky. His uniformed appearance was sharp and newly pressed. The events of the preceding night would have found most men buried in doubt between warm linen sheets at the county hospital, but Joe had work to do. The clock was still running on his time card, and he came back to finish his shift. He swayed on his feet like a boxer waiting for the bell as Coyote coaxed Hillary, his well-built and most reliable wrecker, into position straddling the road. Hillary was a serious truck. Her impressive body was painted a dazzling pearl white with red and green pin striping deftly applied along her curves. She was fitted with enough polished steel to reflect a man's vanity, and her long, muscular boom, stiffened into position in the bed above two axles and a fifth wheel, could lift fifty tons of hardened metal without breaking a sweat. Hillary wouldn't strain a polished nut fishing the light-bodied Diablo out of the water. The yellow and blue strobes on her pylon crown sprayed a perimeter of light that commanded attention, and the husky smell of fuel and rubber announced that this was a man's truck. Shifting the superb vehicle back and forth across the road until he was satisfied with the angle of its placement, Joe's old teammate was another man who wouldn't sleep until the job was wrapped up. He locked on the air brakes, sidled his long, blue-jeaned frame out of the cab, and then slammed a pair of wooden blocks beneath the wheels with a resounding thud from a twenty-pound sledgehammer. With everything situated to his liking, he handed the two iron tow hooks to one of the three wet-suited divers.

"Use both cables so that we can get a good grip on this thing. Let's roll," Coyote said, releasing the thick cable as the diver walked the steel lines down to the pontoon rescue boat. He waited patiently as the three men attached the heavy hooks to the stern, making sure that the two lines cleared the outboard motor.

"Let her go!" the dive leader finally yelled above the diesel growl of Coyote's engine.

Coyote spit a brown wad of tobacco juice into the stones as he slowly engaged his twin planetary winches. He gave the dive leader a snappy salute and enough half-inch cable to do the job. As the men motored slowly away from shore, he turned his attention to Joe, and sang with a woefully challenged timbre.

"Hey Joe, where you goin' with that gun in your hand? I said, hey Joe, where you gonna go now with that gun in your hand. Hey Joe, aooooooo." He howled while tipping his head up to the sky like the toothy beast that he was named after.

Joe just smiled, thinking back to the days when the tall and angular Coyote used to bark at the moon and spit tobacco juice on the field in front of every player who played over him. It wasn't an act of malice as much as it was Coyote's way of marking his turf. That grass belonged to Coyote and the Volunteers, and any poor soul who came to challenge them had to buckle up against the home-field advantage. The brown glop that was oozing at their feet was just a part of it; the Volunteer faithful bringing the noise was the other. No town brought the noise like Toussaint. It was a swell of sound that reverberated out of the stadium and into the surrounding air with enough volume to keep all of the hound dogs barking until morning. Except for his graying mustache and thinning hair, Coyote was the same noisy dog that he had been so many years before, catching passes and rolling wildly around in the end zone after each score, rubbing his scent deeper into the Toussaint field.

"You're the man, Blue," Coyote said, nodding his head. "You're still the man. I ain't seen nothin' like last night. No way, no how, and it ain't likely that I ever will again." Coyote hitched up his jeans as he continued to winch out more cable. "That was the worst storm of my lifetime, maybe of all time. And there you were carryin' that fine-lookin' female out of her watered grave just like you were doin' business as usual." He took a breath and then spit another load of brown goo into the stones. "And look at you. Not a mark on you, and ol' Nate got tore up like a one-legged man in a butt-kickin' contest." He spit again to collect his next point. "I don't know, Blue. I just can't figure it." He stopped talking for a moment as he stuck his right finger into his right ear and jiggled it enough to vibrate the bill of his green ball cap. "Dagnab can't-see-ums!" He cursed as he tilted his head down to the right. "But you say that the hospital checked her out and there was no alcohol?"

"That's right."

"Strange, really strange," Coyote said while removing the remains of the tiny black insect that he had dismembered in his ear, "unbelievably strange." He rolled the words off his tongue while widening his eyes like a faded vampire in a black-and-white movie.

"There's the little bugger." He examined the tip of his finger, and then he flicked the minute body parts toward Joe. "Boo!"

Joe did not flinch. He did not even blink. He just grinned with a slow, one-cornered smile that had fit him since he was a boy. It was unbelievably strange, but strangeness had been stirring his blood with a hot spoon, and this was just one more mystery ingredient for the pot.

The dive team stopped above their dive marker, then signaled to Coyote that two of them were going down. Coyote stopped talking and waited for the next signal. He drained the last good juice from his chew, removed it from his mouth, and flung it into the weeds. Then he reached into his back pocket for a fresh start without losing his concentration on the divers. Plugging the new chew into his left cheek, he continued to inch the lines into the water. His excitement was mounting. He savored the vicarious feeling of power as Hillary trolled the river's bottom for an easy catch. All that he had to do was set the hook and pull. It never failed.

The second signal was given before he was able to work up a good spit. He put the brake to his winches. In a few moments, he could start retrieving the lines. He knew the routine. He had worked with these men before. The three were not Toussaint men, but they were good men all the same. They were confidential men who would not speak about what came up from the bottom unless Joe gave the word. It was just another routine salvage job and nothing more, unless Joe Water said otherwise. The three divers were now back on board their wide-decked craft. The motor man reversed the boat safely away from the cables, then sat idling in the water, curious to see what they had hooked.

"Pull her up!" the dive leader commanded.

Coyote whooped out his trademark howl, gave a brisk salute, spit in the stones, and then slowly engaged the winches to take up the slack. When the cables were evened up, he hit the fast idle and started winching. The cables did not budge. He pulled the lever out into neutral and then slammed it back into gear. Still, the cables did not move. He repeated the motion three times.

"Dagnabbit," he swore while ejecting a brown spray of frustration through his clenched teeth, "this baby never backs out on me!"

"Maybe Hillary's fed up with your nagging." Joe smiled while running his right hand across the back of his neck.

"She loves me!" Coyote shot back as he continued applying the power. The only movement in the river was the rescue boat motoring slowly away from the site. The only movement on the road was the monster truck quaking beneath the strain and Coyote jamming the winches in and out of gear. There was no movement in the lines.

"Judas Priest!" Coyote spit out the words in a wet rush that speckled Hillary's perfect paint job with weeping brown dots. "What are we hooked up to?"

"I think Hillary's had enough," Joe said.

"Never!" Coyote shouted out another spray that misted the air with enough of his tobacco-flavored breath that Joe could smell it from where he stood.

"Calm down, buddy. I'm just reporting what I see." Too much of everything had passed since midnight for Joe Water to be off his game on Twin Bridges this morning. The divers were also on the ball as they continued to distance themselves from the dive marker.

"Come on, girl, dig in! Yank that foreign frog out of our mud!" Coyote wheezed as his voice trailed off breathlessly.

Just as he inhaled for another round of words, Hillary jerked backward over the wheel blocks. While her air brakes blasted out a hissing resistance, the winches kicked in and started reeling cable faster than Coyote could react to disengage them. It was crazy! It was unheard of, and had it been witnessed before, it still would have been unexplainable. It was a toss-up. Either the truck was winching itself into the river or the river was reeling in the truck.

"Good Lord!" Coyote shouted as he held on to the lever, trying desperately to throw the winches out of gear. It was useless. The fight was on! The truck was being dragged toward the river while its locked wheels squealed defiantly, drawing skid-marked objections across the pavement. Coyote swung his long body into the truck bed, bearing his whole weight against the lever. It was futile. The truck continued to lose ground, peeling black skin where the rubber met the road. It struck the guard-rail, bending into it inch by inch with each grinding turn of the winches, popping its taillights, disfiguring the perfect contour of each welded seam on its rear end. As the truck's formidable rear bumper folded inward, the screech of bending steel and the acrid fumes of burnt rubber foretold who would be on the losing end of the struggle if Coyote failed to get a keen hold on the situation. In another few feet, Hillary would be over the side, down the rocky slope, and into the river with the frenzied Coyote clinging madly to the controls. Time, once again, moved against them.

Joe leaped inside the cab and started syncing the clutch and gears together, his muscular limbs gaining control of the six hundred horses of diesel power under the hood. He was throttling up with eighteen gears at his command, but he only needed one to gain an advantage. He eased down on the accelerator pedal as the transmission transferred first-gear power to the twin axles. Two thousand pounds of US tread grabbed the edge of the pavement as the test began between the torque of Coyote's truck, the will of the unseen force, and the man who was now behind the wheel. The motor man quickly spun the dive boat around and sped off to the safety of open water. He understood the hazards of a snapped line. Joe knew as well, but he was holding his ground as Hillary dug in, coughing black smoke from her diesel lungs, tugging on the lines until the winches stalled out. The first time-swallowing moments were a stalemate. Hillary stood still, straining against the stiffened cables, while the wrecked Diablo remained perversely bound to the river's bottom. Something had to give. Joe felt it coming and ordered Coyote off the truck.

"Jump!" he yelled, and Coyote listened, springing off of the truck's bed and running a deep post pattern down the road.

The boom gave first, spewing hydraulic oil into the air as it collapsed upon itself. Joe seized the advantage by jerking the truck forward, taking up the slack from the fallen boom. The sudden progress in motion was encouraging, so Joe applied more throttle to his cause.

"Come on, big girl, you can do it," he said, and the great truck responded. Straining mightily on the cable, her axles started turning and her huge footprint started gripping, and with a little more pedal from Joe, Hillary broke the deadlock with an Amazonian tug. As soon as she started moving, Joe steered her nose north and kept shifting through the gears. He didn't want to lose the advantage. The fight was going his way, and he was running with it.

The Diablo broke through the surface in a breaching, tangled heap. It skidded up the rocky embankment, spinning and twirling, and then hit the road bouncing behind two hundred feet of stressed-out cable, like a sparking ball on a string. Joe continued to shift through the gears. He wanted to put some distance between himself and Twin Bridges. He sped down the road with the bouncing heap in tow until he was satisfied that the river could not take back what it had just surrendered. Then he downshifted slowly and deliberately, keeping the mangled Diablo on a tight leash until coming to a controlled stop. He took a deep, calming breath, relaxed his grip on the wheel, and then waited for Coyote to reclaim his cherished truck.

"Ladies and gentlemen, another ninety-yard score by Toussaint's Bluuuuuue Waaaaaater," Coyote hollered through his cupped hands, creating a stadium's drone, while dancing up to the truck. "Volunteers! Volunteers! Volunteers!" The shouting continued as he ran in place with his own passionate style of exaggerated knee lift. Jutting his arms over his head to signal a touchdown, he was lost in a twenty-year-old memory. "You are the man, Blue Water. You are bulletproof. Better than that, you are bombproof! You…are…the…man. That stinkin' river's got nothin' on you. If the Toussaint won't give it up, then by God, you'll just take it from her. She's a mean ol' bitch, but you, my man, are the number-one stud hound. Honor and glory to you, my friend, you are the one! You are the one! You are the one!" he continued screaming while running in place with both hands held straight up in the air, pointing toward the heavens, jubilant with the notion of unforgotten things.

Joe felt pleasure in the evenness of his life as he watched the unchanged Coyote still dancing in tune with his old high school steps. He was pleased, but no longer confident that it would always be this way. Today was a different day. The events were not organized in his mind. He could feel himself moving away from his center, drifting into places that had free-falling limits. It was a day for remembering that things could change if a man wasn't paying attention. He checked his rearview mirror to see what entity of change might be creeping up on him.

"What's the matter, Blue?" Coyote asked as he reached inside the cab to wrap his skinny arm around Joe's thick neck.

"Do you smell that?" Joe asked calmly.

"Smell what?"

Puzzled by the aromatic flavor that wrapped itself around his senses, Joe was serious with his question. "Smell the air. It's so sweet that I can taste it."

Coyote let go of Joe's neck, stuck his nose into the morning breeze, and sniffed at it like a hound following a scented trail. "Yeah, I smell it now. It smells like a quality woman, all sweet and clean and waitin' for a good lickin'."

"That's not the smell of a woman."

"My sniffer might be a little out of shape, Blue. It's been so long since I breathed in a good woman that this ol' dog may have lost the scent."

"The smell doesn't belong here. It's not familiar to this place."

"Neither is my dream woman, but she might have passed through here last night." Coyote laughed, giving the air another sniff. "It's just the river, Chief, and there's nothin' sweet about that water." He stepped off of the running board and shook his head from side to side. "It's just the river."

Joe was not convinced. He stuck his head out of the window to get a good look over his shoulder, and then he opened the door and walked away from the truck. He looked straight down the highway, examining the water on both sides of Twin Bridges. The road was clear, the marshland was serene, and Joe was feeling tired.

"Reel in your catch, Coyote, and haul it back home. I'll give it another look when it's in the yard.

We have to open this road back up and get the traffic moving, and one more thing, I'm sorry about Hillary. I hope that you can fix her bruises."

"I can fix most anything, Chief."

"Agreed, let's get busy, and then we can call it a day." Joe knew this to be true, at least most of the time.

After the cleanup was completed, Joe called off the roadblock, logged out with the dispatcher, and then headed home. Change was coming slowly to Joe Water, and he knew that it was coming for Toussaint. He caught its scent, and he could feel its presence. His shift was finally over, but his real work had just begun. He was going home to sleep on it.

Chapter 4

Joe Water's home was a relic even for Toussaint, where all past things were held tight enough to draw blood. The simple cabin had been built by Joe's pioneering ancestors after the French voyagers arrived in 1615 on All Saints' Day and named the marshland Toussaint, in honor of the many spirits that protected them. There was no witness to the day the Water clan arrived, and only a whisper of where they had come from. They easily adapted to both the wild and civilized elements around them and needed nothing but their own hard work to survive. They were so still about their coming and going that the whole line of them lived and died and their ashes were spread from corner to corner across the verdant wetlands with only family members present to testify. They left nothing behind them but this centuries-old cabin that was uncomplicated and built to last, much like the man who lived inside. It was situated on the wet prairie above Turtle Creek, overlooking the rich bog that was teeming with all but human life. It was the only private structure allowed to stand within the fertile miles of government-protected shoreline that stretched between the eastern boundary beyond Magee Marsh and the western boundary waters of the Ottawa National Wildlife Refuge. When the Division of Wildlife claimed domain over this untamed area, the Water homestead was permitted to remain private until the day that it would no longer be occupied by a Water kin. It was the family home for each generation of the Water bloodline, of which, according to record, Joe was the sole member still standing.

Joe Water's naked body was pressed wearily into the flannel sheets on top of his mattress. He rarely covered himself with human or bedclothes when he slept, and this day was no different. He was breathing the deep sleep when Nathan Swift pounded his familiar rap upon the door. Joe usually awoke from his sleep without an alarm, stirred by his own internal clock. It was a discipline that he had practiced without error since he was a child. He could give himself an exact hour or any number of odd minutes of sleep, and he would always rise on time. Odd numbers suited him best, especially those that were prime, standing alone, divisible only by one or itself. Joe was up and rolling at twenty-one thirteen. By twenty-two thirteen he was stretched, fed, showered, pressed, and good to go. He was always on the road thirty-seven minutes before he was on the clock, but this day would be different by that standard. This day was going to start on Nate's watch.

Within seconds of his friend's drumming on the door, Joe was standing barefoot in front of him, dressed in baggy pants and a smile. It was in stark contrast to the starched appearance that usually covered him with his official duty. Out of uniform, anyone could see just how much his skin was built for him, wrapped around his hard-cut features in tight angles and curves that flexed and flowed like a river through rock. His skin was his armor, the iron shirt that was forged in the fire of his youth. He was capable of moving through anything if it stayed in his way long enough. It was no problem to associate this same man with the celebrated figure who still ran off tackle in the minds of those who refused to forget. It was easy for them to still see that boy walking around in this man's body; this man who stood shirtless in the doorway looked unchanged by time, experience, or the stock moods of men. His manner and bearing were common only to Joe Water and could never be confused with those who tried to fit inside his walk or copy his delivery.

Filling the open doorway, Nate was authoritatively dressed and ready for work. "Your tour has almost started, Blood. It's not like you to be sacked out this close to roll call."

"You look good, buddy. It was tough getting that extra yard last night." Joe grinned as he looked at Nate's newly stitched face beneath the distinctive brim of his trooper's hat.

"As usual, the Good Lord was looking out for you, Blue. I pray hard to be heard, but he hears your need first."

"I don't know what to tell you, buddy boy. I must be living a charmed life."

"God only knows, Blue. Someone's looking over your shoulder, that's for sure. Are you going to let me in?"

"Sorry, buddy, I was just admiring your new look. Come on in, and we'll throw down some coffee and talk about it."

"Have you taken any calls since you hauled her vehicle out of the river?" Nate asked as he stepped inside the house.

Joe pulled a scruffy red T-shirt over his head, with "Volunteer Football" a not-so-faded memory stretched across his chest. "No, I told my crew to keep a lid on everything until I got some sleep."

"Well, the lid blew off, Blood." Nate removed his trooper's hat and then closed the door behind him.

The inside of Joe's small home spoke more of who he was rather than who he had been. Spartan, masculine, and spit-shine clean, every wall was white and void of the usual vanities of a man's history, especially a man such as Joe Water, a man who stood out among other men's glorious tales of what used to be. The floors were hewn from native timber with a hard, polished surface and a tough grain that had mellowed little throughout the years. The door to an empty bedroom was open. The only object in the room was a small branch from a bristlecone pine tree that held a venerable position on the exact center of the floor. A single window framed the eastern horizon. In the sitting room, a legal pad fixed to a clipboard shared the top of an old handmade table with a police radio, a telephone, and seven wooden pencils placed in perfect rank according to length. Apart from the wooden chair at the table, there was no other furniture in the room. The house was immaculate and free of pretense. Joe's bedroom was concealed behind a closed door.

They moved through the house and went directly into the kitchen. Nate immediately sat down in one of the four wooden chairs that were grouped around a small drop-leaf table. Much of their life had passed between deep cups of dark coffee, with both elbows up on this same tabletop. More real talk was delivered here than could be found in any other gathering in Toussaint. It was clean, precise, respectful talk that was absent of entitlement and delivered without hidden meaning. It was the kind of honest talk that only the truest of brothers could speak. It was the kind of incorruptible talk that inspired them to serve and protect their people. Before it was spoken, Joe Water poured a thick fog-lifter that could make a dead man walk. They added nothing to the brew but their thoughts.

"What's on your mind, Nate?" Joe asked, seating himself across the table from the only man who knew him off the record.

"I stopped by at the boneyard to check out the wreckage and—"

"This is Toussaint," Joe interrupted. "The state has no call on this."

Nate looked down at his reflection in the black surface of his drink. "It wasn't official, Blue. You know better. Have you taken a good look at yourself?"

Joe knew straightaway where Nate was heading. If there were ever differences between them, it was Nate who peeled them back with clear revelation. Joe did not answer.

"What are the odds that you could live through that storm without a scratch, and how about that young angel that you walked out of the marsh with? She didn't have a flaw anywhere on her body, not one imperfection, and they gave her more than a once-over look at the hospital. We all did!"

Joe shrugged his heavyweight shoulders. "So… did you like what you saw?"

"Come on, brother man, you saw her. Do you have to ask?"

Joe stared at Nate with brown-eyed awareness. "Just checking your pulse, buddy."

Calmly lifting up his pummeled face to offer it for inspection, Nate gave Joe more than enough to consider. "Well I'm still alive, and I thank God for that, but we all three took the same pounding in that wind-fire, and I'm the only one who got burned."

Joe did not have to examine him too closely. The evidence of the bizarre night was written all over Nate's face in deep bruises and punctured skin. Joe knew that his friend was going to have questions, but he also knew that he couldn't provide any answers, so he just took a long taste of his coffee and settled his back into the hard chair.

Nate continued to drive. "There's something else, Blood. Her car is just a memory."

"A memory?"

"Affirmative, it vanished off the hook like a live one slipping over the side. Coyote swears that it was chained to his truck and the yard was locked down and tended to by those junkyard dogs of his before he went into the garage to sleep off this morning's excitement. Nobody could enter or leave that yard without dealing with those hellhounds, but when Coyote woke up, the dogs were calm, the yard was still locked up, but the vehicle was gone." Nate reached his right hand down the front of his tight collar, grasped his gold crucifix, and then put it to his mouth and kissed it. "The good Lord himself would have been troubled to keep quiet in that yard." Then he caressed the tiny gold figure on the cross between his thumb and index finger as he tucked it back into its faithful place above his heart.

Nate's ritual was always satisfying to Joe. It was something that he could rely on, something that was permanent in his friend's thinking. "I guess a lot can happen while a man sleeps."

"So it seems, Blue, but that's not the end of it. Word is that she was drinking stiff ones all night at Violet's."

"I've heard."

"She drank more than a good man could hold."

"I know."

Nate held his left hand up and raised one finger for each point that he was making. "She was perfect inside and out when they examined her at the hospital, not a scratch on her and a zero-percent blood alcohol level. She was as right of mind and body as a woman could be, and when the ER released her, she politely walked a straight line out the door and out of sight."

"I know."

Nate switched over to his right hand as he continued his case. "Did you also know that the hospital has no record of her treatment, not even her name?"

"That's their business."

"Affirmative, I'll give you that, but do you know why they don't have her record?"

"Let me guess. It just disappeared, and only God knows what happened to it?"

"That's right, Blood, whatever personal facts they had just vanished into thin air. God knows for sure, but what about you? Do you still have her information?"

"Joe tapped the rim of his cup seven times with his right index finger. "You don't have to start counting on your toes. It's all in my report."

"Maybe you should give that report another look, Blue?"

Joe set his cup down on the table and then walked out to the sitting room to review the report on his clipboard. To his surprise, the writing pad was blank; the record had been wiped clean of this woman. Joe examined the pad, carefully turning every page over in his hand, searching for clues to this mystery, but there were none to find. The pad was as clean and unwritten upon as the day he placed it into service. No smudges, no marks, almost sterile-looking.

"Nothing," Joe sighed as he placed the clipboard back on the table. He was uneasy, less sure of the details, and it wore on him like a stone in his boot. He just wasn't ready to shake it out. He returned to the kitchen empty-handed and sat back down at the kitchen table.

"Well, Blood, do you have her name?"

"I did, but I don't have it anymore."

"Do you even remember it?"

"Her name doesn't matter. She wasn't charged with anything, so there's no reason to remember her name."

"Forget her name! Would you even recognize her face? Do you remember what she looked like?"

"No..."

"Do you remember anything about her?"

"Not much..."

"Not much, brother man? That's what I'm saying. Every other thing about last night is remembered point by point, but nobody is clear about the woman who caused it all."

Joe leaned away from the table and started rocking on the back legs of his chair. "She didn't bring the storm."

"From your mouth to God's ear. Can you be certain, Blue?"

"Don't be a crazy Indian."

"I'm no crazier than what you're probably thinking, but not saying. This might be the biggest thing that has ever landed on Toussaint's doorstep, and our memory of it is just as murky as the black ooze on the river bottom. The easiest, simplest thought is that there was a storm and Chief Water did his job. Is that how it goes down?"

"I guess so."

"I guess not, Blood, and neither do you. This situation is going to sit over you and camp out. This is your town, brother, and the folks need you to answer them. You're going to make dust or eat dust. Times are changing, the world's closing in around us, and I'm hearing the word outside of Toussaint."

"What's the word, Nate?"

"God bless you, Blood, but be advised; the word is that Blue Water answers to no one but himself."

"What's that supposed to mean?"

"Come on, Blood, you had better get in step before the dogs start running up on your heels."

Joe fixed his blue eye on his friend's face. "Don't let them think for you. It's bad enough that they have robbed you of your skin."

"Nobody has robbed me. I step freely where it is free to step."

"Oh brother! You look good when you're dancing in your moccasins, but the priest's collar clashes with that uptight state uniform. What's going on inside your own head, buddy? Why the urgency in your voice? What are you thinking right now? "

"What do I think? I think this is bigger than me, bigger than Toussaint, bigger than everything outside of Toussaint, and God help us if it's bigger than you. Last night was not random. It had purpose and design. That storm was hellacious, and it blew into town with a mind-numbing, unforgettable female who remains forgotten. She has vanished like a vapor, with her vehicle and every record of her existence. All that we know for sure is that she ended up in your arms, alive and kicking in the rut of the storm, after taking a high dive into the river. It makes your heart race, doesn't it? Now you tell me, Blue, what do you think?"

The silence between them was thick and deep as they listened to each other breathing in the air of unfamiliar thoughts. Joe was struggling with his memory, trying to add detail to the rough edges of forgotten things. He remembered how light had gathered around her face, even in the terrible darkness of the storm. He contemplated her luminous eyes, yet he could not recall their color. He was confounded by her vital and unmarked state and bewildered by his own similar condition. He could still feel the sensation of her cold and lifeless body at the bottom of the river, and he was wrestling with the epiphany that had saved them both. He had no words for his friend, at least none that would answer the questions that were thrown on the table. He sat straight up against the back of his chair, looked past Nate, and focused only on the ancient limb that balanced his life.

"I was sleeping," Joe said, breaking the long, unsettling silence.

Nate raised his eyebrows, tightening the stitches in his head. "You were sleeping?"

"Affirmative, I was sleeping."

"Affirmative, that's all you've got. You were sleeping?"

"Confirmed, I was sleeping, but now I'm awake. Protect the perimeter, Nate, and I will take care of everything between the ends. This is no different than any other game plan, buddy."

"Don't bet on it, Blue."

"I don't bet on it; I count on it." Joe braced his forearms on top of the table as he folded his hands together. Nate did the same, hands clasped, eyeball to eyeball with Joe.

"It's just like the Old One used to say: the immortal Blue Water—too good to be human, too bad not to be! You're done talking aren't you, Blood?"

"I won't be writing a book about it."

"This story has already been written. What you have here, Blood, is just one more chapter, and it may be the last. Before you go on shift tonight, stop over to Violet's Friendly Tavern and see for yourself."

"Whose vision of things should I use, your eyes or mine?"

"You'll see what I mean. This time is different. I don't think that you will be closing the book on this one anytime soon."

"I doubt it," Joe quickly replied.

Of all the words that Joe could have spoken, these last three revealed everything to Nate. If there was a constant in Joe Water's life, it was that he never doubted anything that he did. He was always straightforward and headfirst into every situation. If there was a crack developing in his sureness, Nathan Swift would be the first to recognize it. *"I doubt it"* said more about himself than Joe had ever intended to tell.

"All right, Blue, but this is what's brewing up over there. You are the only soul capable of getting everyone to agree that no evidence exists."

"There is no crime, Nate, so there is no evidence to be collected," Joe said firmly.

"I agree with you on that, Blood, but where's the record? You always keep a record. It's standard operating procedure, and Lord knows that Blue always crosses his t's and dots his i's. Nobody that I know is more obsessed with detail than you."

"I'm not obsessed. I'm thorough. What's with the cross-examination? Are you bucking for prosecutor in the next election?"

"I'm on your side, Blue, not the devil's side. This has the appearance of a secret that's just too big for the rest of us to know. Last night, Blue Water was clean and flowing, but today, Blue Water runs outside of town on a pale horse that only listens to his master's voice."

Joe stared at Nate's messed-up looks and serious expression and started laughing. His laughter was loud and infectious, and Nate caught it. They laughed long and hard, coughing out the rowdy noise of friends. Nate could always make Joe laugh, even when he was being stone-faced serious. Joe reached across the table and grabbed Nate behind the head, gripping him solidly where his neck was the reddest, and then shook him playfully like a bobblehead doll.

"I love your Indian sense of things, Nate, even if I'm the only one who understands it."

Nate twisted out of Joe's grasp. "I am Shawnee, doggone it. If you want to shake an Indian, go up to the hospital and give one of the doctors a headache."

"I'm sorry, brother, I do know the difference." Joe shifted his hips as he apologized. "But you really are one funny Shawnee."

"Isn't that the pot calling the kettle black? Someday I'm going to take that stick of yours back to where it belongs. Then your world will really get funny. Without that crutch, you'll be a two-legged man."

"I am a two-legged man," Joe laughed. "See, brother, you just can't help yourself. You are a mixed-up mongrel of a Shawnee, neither wolf nor dog."

Nate rubbed the prominent tip of his chin with his right hand, trying to squeeze the smile out of his face, but it was useless. They both broke out into a fit of laughter that lasted until the humor settled back into the seat of important things. As the night cut down the daylight on the first day after the storm, that which was left unanswered would turn to others to gain some life.

"It's time to roll, Nate. Thanks for the wake-up call."

Nate pushed himself away from the table. "No problem, I've got you covered. Keep your nose to the wind, Blue. It's blowing your way."

Joe remained quiet until they reached the front door. Placing both of his hands on the top of Nate's head, he spoke softly. "Always…You'll heal, brother. Don't worry about a thing."

"Do I need to worry?"

"Never…"

"Keep me posted, Blood."

"Always," Joe repeated before closing the door behind his friend.

Even though the clock was pressing him to quicken his pace, Joe Water walked into the empty room and stood over the ancient cut of wood on the floor. He reached down and touched the antediluvian branch that he simply called "the stick." He touched it in a way that offered respect as only he could understand, witnessing the message of this primordial sprig of truth. It was a borrowed branch of the great bristlecone pine tree that the Shawnee Prophet called The Great Wonder. White men who had only heard of its existence called it the Methuselah tree because it was the oldest known living thing in the world. It grew in a secret place, on sacred ground in the Sierra Nevada Mountains of California. Passed down to Joe through the hands of the Old One, who knew its meaning, the stick bore out the scars of more than four thousand years of drawing life from the earth. Touching the stick, Joe recognized that it had lived before the great religions of the world took root on different ground. This was the legitimacy of The Great Wonder, the reality that made the stick superior to any contrived divinity that only materialized in the surreal minds of mankind. Locked within the branch were the intact memories of its entire lifetime. Written within the chemical history of each cell was the living record of each day of its existence. It was real, and it was wonderful in its exactness. Those who witnessed this obvious fact about the tree could also experience each day for what it really was, not for what it promised to be. Joe accepted this uncomplicated awareness as his supreme truth, and he applied it to everything under the sun; possessed by each universal thing is the memory of its lifetime, the secret of its being, and the proof of its purpose. It was enough religion for him. Joe Water was a man of great faith. He believed in himself, he believed in his friends, and he believed in Toussaint. If there was a better man standing, he wasn't standing where anyone could see him.

As the moon rose over Toussaint, one by one, couple by couple, the regulars made their way over to Violet's Friendly Tavern. From the fields and the factories, they came to speak beyond the usual talk. Between each lifted bottle and emptied glass, they typically spoke in low tones about all that was and sometimes all that could have been, but on this night, the conversation was loud, and the talk was all about what might be coming.

The atmosphere sparked with the static charge of confusion, but when Joe Water entered the bar, the air stopped moving. Every drinker except Violet Love cast their eyes to the nearest bottle while their exhaled puffs of tobacco smoke made their way, unchallenged by breath or sound, to the high ceiling. Spreading itself across the top of the room in a moving, curling mass, the rarefied cloud of smoke was the only thing in motion except for Violet; continuing to wipe down the bar top, she had her huckleberry eyes on Joe as he eyed everything else. If a pin had dropped, it would have sounded as thunder. The seconds were longer than time intended them to be, long enough for Joe to see what he had come to see. It was indeed as Nate had spoken. A silent room at Violet's could only mean one thing. They were talking about the last man to enter the bar, and there was nobody else standing behind Joe. He rolled his left shoulder, and then his right, shook the blood down to the fingers of both hands, and then turned and walked out the door. Arriving at his cruiser in slow, deliberate steps, he had a lot on his mind when he called in for his shift.

"Dispatcher, this is Water. I'm on the job and heading due north on Route Nineteen. Log me in."

There was no response.

"Dis-pat-cher," he called a second time, dividing the word into three commanding syllables, "this is Water. I'm heading due north on Nineteen. Log me in."

There was still no response.

"Dispatcher!" He now pronounced the word firmly into one demand. "Wake up and take the call!"

"Sorry, Chief," the dispatcher stammered, "I'll round that up to an even ten thirty p.m."

"Negative," Joe called back. "The time is twenty-two twenty-seven. Every second stands for something, son. Count it all."

"Affirmative, Chief, the time is duly noted."

"That's better, son. Before you sign off tonight, talk to Dispatcher Marshall about timekeeping."

"Affirmative, Chief, will do. I'm sorry about that. It won't happen again."

"No sweat, son, I believe in you."

"Thank you, sir, I believe in you too."

Debbie Marshall was just entering the office when she overheard the communication. She walked over to the rookie dispatcher who was manning the afternoon shift and laid a kindly hand on his young shoulder. "The Chief is synchronized and in touch with every hour. If you can remember that, it will keep him happy, and your records will muster up in court," she said with a reassuring pat on his back.

"Does he care about every second?" the rookie asked.

"Like an atomic clock."

"What if you're caught between minutes? Do you round up or down?"

"The Chief is always ahead of the game. Keep moving the clock forward, and you will most likely catch up to him."

"Thank you, Mrs. Marshall." He stood up politely to offer his chair.

"Thank you. Your mother taught you well." She sat down with an elegant grace as she readied herself for work.

"Have you heard the talk, ma'am?"

"Yes," she quickly replied.

"Well, what do you think?"

"We get paid around here to take the calls, not to make them. If you don't mind, I would appreciate it if you would start me a fresh pot of coffee before you log out."

"Yes, ma'am, I'll remember that. You like your coffee strong, don't you?"

"Strong, black, and quiet with just a taste of sugar," she said smiling.

Joe Water was caught in the dark as much as those who were bending elbows at Violet's Friendly Tavern. The only light that was shed on the road ahead was the bright sweep of white that emanated from his cruiser's headlights. Other than that, the only thing that was clear in his mind as he approached the railroad tracks was the county cleanup, where the orange vests worked overtime to replace the busted crossing gates and clear the roads of windblown debris. He liked it when those who were on the payroll earned their money by finishing the job on time; it was the most honest thing to do.

Joe resented the image of the yellow Speed Kills sign as it entered his peripheral vision. Remembering when the athletic boosters erected it during his senior season of football, he thought of it as a final mocking good-bye to Volunteer opponents as they limped out of town, licking their wounds. Unlike the boosters, Joe did not like the cheap shot to the ribs. To him, it was spreading the salt, and he didn't think a man gained anything by pouring it into an open wound. It bothered his unassuming nature even more when Nate's name and his name were added to the insult, becoming the axiom for

Volunteer football throughout Ohio. The headlines didn't vary much as the Volunteers worked their way down to the state title. They were always some worn combination of "Speed Kills," "Swift-Water Rushes," "Swift-Water Pours," or "Swift-Water Storms Over Their Opponent." Joe never believed any of the puffed-up print or the bragging voices of his past, but all the same, they were as much a part of him as the road beneath his wheels. Good or bad, once something was established in Toussaint, the memories were carried forever.

As he accelerated beyond the tracks, he saw the same scene that he always passed on this road. The houses, mailboxes, barns, and farmhouses were standing where they always stood. The machine shop, the bait shop, the grain elevator, and the fields that would soon be flush with soybeans and maize remained constant. If there were changes made along this road, it was a secret to all but those who kept it. For this reason, Toussaint was his world. He liked the way that things were. Except for the rare silence at Violet's Friendly Tavern, he had no reason to feel otherwise. The silence was not a threat; it was only a question to be answered.

Joe knew that Nate would start to interpret the events with the cryptic methodology of his adopted

Christian tradition. Nate, like every soul in the village limits, trusted God to send signs that he was moving through their lives. They were not fanatical to the point of worshipping rusty stains that appeared on the village water tower, or seeing illusory icons in their morning cereal, but they were visual seekers who would be quick to interpret the extraordinary happenings as more supernatural than explicable. Joe felt that Nate was just talking the talk of those who took him in as their own. He also knew that Nate's God-fearing, spook-driven soul could never completely dilute his Shawnee blood. While he prayed to God, he still had the sixth sense of his ghost-dancing ancestors, fearless warriors who had died in the physical world but had substance in the ethereal universe of the mind. That's why Joe trusted him, loved him, and held him as a brother. Nate was much like the ancient stick, and he was much like Joe. They were both the products of their own time, the products of all time. They held the answers to their living within their experiences and nothing more. Nate was fearless because he believed that death would be good to him, Joe because death could not hold him. In the meantime, they were just trying to keep the peace and protect their people.

Joe made his way to Twin Bridges. He pulled his cruiser into the stones where the fishermen from Toledo sometimes hung lanterns on forked sticks and fished the weed beds beneath the night sky. Anytime he saw the white glow beaming along the shoreline, he would stop and ask about their luck. They would exchange tips about their bait and lures and also about jigging along the structure. When they ran out of pointers, they would banter on about their greatest catch of all time. Joe never won the tale of the biggest fish; he always told the truth.

When he turned off his headlights, the pitch-black darkness was void of all illumination but the reflected surface of the moon. Cold and empty, there would be no fish stories to swap tonight. Joe exited his vehicle spreading his handheld light through the stillness that surrounded him. He walked with purpose in a remembered cadence that had rhythm and meaning beyond the usual steps of men. This night after the storm gave him reason to do so. He worked his way up to the circle of disfigured cottonwoods that bent leeward toward the point, where the eastern blows created a permanent yield of bowed and suffering vegetation. The rigid and the flexible alike shared the fate of the bent and broken. Nothing had been spared from the wrath of the storm, as even the tall, young grasses revealed the wilted spines of the old and infirm. The entire crop of the land had the appearance of having been stepped on by a mighty shoe.

Joe scanned his light across the moonlit vista of swampy backwater. The nocturnal breeze blew sharply across his face and then made its way through the grasses, frosting each blade as it heaved through marsh and meadow. The river's surface shuddered beneath the frigid wind, breaking into bitter strokes against the rocky shore and then fading back to break once more. Somewhere beyond the blue-green glow of the glimmering fox fire, a solitary common loon wept a lonesome wail that rose and fell in a mindless moan. Joe loved the manic sound of the eerie cry as the bird lurked beyond that which could be seen.

"Crazy as a loon" is a misnomer, he thought. *It's like giving credit to an owl's intellect by judging the human set of its eyes.* He was wondering if such flawed wisdom was all that any man had to rely on. Then, beyond all of that which was occurring in the natural way of things, he heard the rattle of the midnight east-bound rumbling toward the village. It was on time; Joe appreciated such things.

After repeated lighted sweeps of the area, Joe turned off his lamp. He stood motionless, inhaling the night air in long, whispering breaths, his straight body a stark angle to all of the vegetation that bent hopelessly to the west. He was trying to fit in, yet the material line of his physical form betrayed him as one who did not belong. Among plant or beast, Joe Water stood alone. It was his right of birth.

"Blue Water," the voice called out from nowhere.

Joe remained still, thinking that it was a trick of nature.

"Blue Water," the voice called again with a resonance that commanded attention.

Joe did not move.

"Blue Water," the voice called out a third time.

Joe did not blink or take a breath.

"Stand still and listen!"

His sensibilities were being tested. He stood without a twitch. The voice did not have a point of origin. It swept over him from every direction like the sound of air clapping forcefully against each ear after a lightning strike to the top of the head. It was the same sound that had lifted him into the sky the night before. It was the sound of all things calling his name. So he stood still, and he listened, but all that followed was the beating of his own heart. It was loud enough to be carried away on the wind.

After standing motionless for what seemed like the eternal moment, Joe turned his lamp back on and slowly scanned the darkness that surrounded him. Nothing had changed. There was no one to see, no one to question, no one to put in plain words what was going on. Apart from the sweet fragrance that seemed to trail each disordered occurrence, there was no other evidence to corroborate the event. Proof was the trump card of his trade. Without it he was holding an empty hand. An edgy feeling moved across his skin like the uncertain chill of a childhood nightmare, back when his bones were stretching and his muscles were getting firm and taking shape. It was the reason that he slept naked. His T-shirt used to wrap so tightly around his neck that he would wake from his dreams in a frantic sweat, gasping for air. His nakedness gave him freedom from his dusky tossing. His nakedness had brought him peace when sleep was but a restless turning of his young mind. He was no longer unsettled about whom he was, but like the stick, he was never far from who he had been. It all meant something. Without proof, it meant something more than he could understand, at least for the moment.

Chapter 5

Had Joe been an ecclesiastical kinsman to the Toussaint majority, he would have been down on his knees trembling before all that he had experienced. Instead, the wheels were turning in his mind, trying to spin substance from the vaporous mist of the unfathomable. Before tonight, his commandments were written by erudition, not by illusion. He founded his faith upon the dynamics of the natural universe. The code was simple; man was a force of nature whose own conduct determined the dynamic course of his life. Now, he was heading into a dimension of living that defied the application of all that he had known. It was new ground that lacked the firm characteristics of cause and effect. The only direction to take that made sense to him was to walk back to his cruiser, through the darkness that confounded him.

Joe knew that there were uncertainties in life that played their hand against the time that he lived in. He felt that he could not prepare for everything, but he could deal with anything as long as he moved with deliberate purpose. As he turned his cruiser back onto the highway, he recalled such times. He remembered when he ran the ball for the Volunteers, running without conscious effort, without predisposing his body to do something that it could do on its own. He was spellbound when he ran, churning and spinning through the opposing line, feeling nothing but the impulse to drive forward. Any hand that was laid upon him was obscure. No blow delivered the kind of pain that he could feel. Even when he came crashing to the ground beneath the pile-driving impact of a tackler's flesh, he felt nothing but the temporary halt of his forward progress. He could not even hear the wild cheering that aroused the senses of everyone but himself. When Joe was running, moving, cutting left and right, smashing into bone and flesh, muscle to muscle, he was only aware of the sweat that salted his vision. It was a passion that left great stretches of blank space in an otherwise keenly sharpened mind. After the games, when the local news-bees interviewed him, he had little to add to what they saw. When the questions were raised about what he was thinking, or feeling, about a particular moment in the game, his answer was always the same: *"I tried my best. I just ran the ball,"* and he was telling the truth.

There was also a time, a hair-raising moment, when he instantly judged three other living souls as not being fit for life. Twenty years had passed since Joe cut down three outsiders who had Violet beaten and choking on the barroom floor. It was long after closing time, and Violet would not let herself go without a fight. She was delirious and close to death when the rookie patrolman stepped into the scene unarmed. Two of the men attacked him with fixed-blade combat knives as a third gunman stood over a semiconscious Violet with his eye split open and nose bleeding profusely from her enraged defense. Joe struck down one attacker with a skull-breaking fist to the face. The second attacker was cleanly cut through the stomach with his own knife and gutted, before splashing to the floor in his own putrid waste. The gunman had time to raise his Glock 19 only to have the barrel turned in on him and fifteen rounds delivered into his chest, which smeared his seedy leftovers across the back wall. It happened so quickly that Joe could not recollect his course of action. Violet could only bring to mind a blurred Joe Water, the sound of tearing flesh, and the steaming smell of warm blood and muddy boots.

There were no tears shed for the departed. The investigation had ended on Joe's word that he did the best with what was presented to him. Everyone agreed that the kills were righteous, and neither doubt nor sorrow was left behind for anyone to wrestle with. When Joe finished with his work, Toussaint breathed easier, secrets were kept, and Joe buried his memory with the dead; it was easy. With life and death compressed into a fistful of vengeance, he had nothing good to recall except saving what he loved. There was no doubt that he loved Toussaint and the thickness of its rural skin. When the village chief retired, Joe was rewarded with the job. He was the youngest chief of police on record in the state of Ohio.

Joe wheeled around Toussaint throughout the early morning hours without further personal or official incident. He was hoping that the end of his shift would be uneventful, but the season was still open on wild turkey, and that could present a problem. At one half hour before sunrise, the hunters would be stalking the fields to make their seasonal bag limits. Joe was sure about Toussaint's gun-toting offspring, but he was uneasy about outside hunters treading through Toussaint's glory. He was traveling along the east-west boundary road north of Lacarpe Creek, where the railroad tracks and tangled fields provided good habitat for feathered game. He knew that city hunters would be prowling this fertile ground at first light. They would be easy to spot with their orange vests and loudmouthed hats that boasted of colleges that were never attended and stock car numbers that were never earned. Joe wanted to announce his presence to those who were anxious to take aim in the cover of Toussaint's fields. His appearance to outsiders was imperative during their harvest of Toussaint's bounty.

Just as sunup was breaking over the lake, he witnessed the first muzzle flash of the morning, followed by the clear report of a twelve-gauge shotgun blast. Within seconds he saw another flash booming out of the half-lit sky. Both shots were fired by a single hunter with an unmistakable swagger as he turned his hounds loose to fetch the kill. Joe heard a third explosion and then witnessed Coyote falling to the ground with a halo of smoke and fire crawling up his leg. Before the dogs could pick up the bloody scent of their fallen master, Joe was already at his side, stopping the gory flow.

"Jesus, Blue," Coyote stammered as warm steam rose from his mangled limb. "My God, is my leg still there?"

"The first kill of the day had to be notched by you, didn't it, buddy boy," Joe said, drawing Coyote's attention away from his wound.

"Jesus, Blue, what are you talking about? I can't feel my leg!"

"Stop howling," Joe said calmly, squeezing his hands around Coyote's torn flesh as a pulse of red-and-blue light spread urgently through the misty air.

It was Nate's patrol car materializing with the light of dawn. There was no call sent on the air, so whatever brought Nate was either pure luck or providential. He bounced his cruiser through the freshly seeded field, smashing the budding heads of new growth beneath his wheels. He stopped within a footstep of Joe and bolted from the car into the filmy veil of the new day. Even in the dusky strains of refracted light, Nate's face beamed like polished steel. Whatever hand had marked him, another had taken away. His formerly bruised and battered expression was supplanted by a glorious healing that removed years from his excited grin.

"Praise God! Praise the Almighty Lord!" Nate screamed with revivalist fervor. "Look at me, Blood! Look at me good. You have the gift! Jesus, you are the man!"

Joe ignored the praise, but couldn't deny the transformation.

"Jesus, Jesus, Joseph, and Mary, you have the gift! You have the gift!"

"Relax, Nate, you're barking up the wrong tree," Joe said.

"The wrong tree, I don't think so! Look at me, Blue. When I started my shift, I looked like a topo map of Muddy Creek. Now look at me. I've got nothing, Blood, not a scratch, not a bruise, nothing!"

Joe continued to apply the pressure to Coyote's leg as he examined Nate's fresh look.

"Just relax, buddy. I'm working here."

Nate stepped back and took it all in, and what he saw favored what he believed. Coyote's two fierce canine protectors flanked Joe in a stoic manner that was eerily uncommon. Joe was down on his knees, pressing his hands into Coyote's flesh, while the dazed shooter rested as still as a pained man could tolerate without a needle in the hip. Beneath Joe's grasp, Coyote's pant leg was completely shredded; the ground beneath him ran wet with blood. Expecting the sight of ripped flesh and shattered bone, he was instead met with the pale hue of Coyote's hairless skin. As far as Nate could tell, if Coyote had been blasted in the leg by steel bird shot, Joe's touch had just cured the pain and confirmed the situation to be, at the very least, out of the ordinary, if not a true miracle.

"What happened here?" Nate asked, gathering his composure.

"Coyote caught a backfire from his old pepper-gun. Call the paramedics to give us a hand."

"Your hands are enough, Blue. If he took a hit, where's the damage?" He fell to his knees and searched under and over Coyote's body with his hands. "I see the blood all around him, but he isn't bleeding? A twelve gauge at close range would have mangled his leg. I see the blood, but where is the wound?"

Joe looked down at Coyote's perfectly healed limb, and then he looked back to Nate, then again to Coyote. His thoughts were like loose mercury in a hot skillet. He was trying to make sense of a senseless situation, trying to stay straight under the bending pressure of their changing lives. Whatever hand was applying the force now had Nate and Coyote in its grasp. Joe had no idea what had just taken place, but there were two more witnesses to confirm that it happened. He slowly inhaled the sweet air; the remembered taste of it collected his senses into one reasonable breath. In the controlled manner in which he dealt with all things outside of himself, he calmly appealed to them to let it go, at least for now.

"I don't understand what this all means, but I will find an answer, and you two will be the first to know. If either of you speak of what you think just happened, I'm going to have two thousand citizens camped out on my land, burning candles and chanting hymns. We have to be on the same page with this, or it will grow beyond our ability to control. Nate, don't go to the post to log out tonight. Go directly home. Do not speak to anyone about what you might be thinking, even if you believe that what you are thinking is a good thing to know. Take a sick leave, maybe a week or two. Keep out of sight. Folks will understand, given your condition last night. Coyote, you do the same. Go home and stay home until I get back to you. Can you do this for me? Can you do this for all of us?"

Nate and Coyote were mute. Had there ever been a second when either of them were struck dumb by unknown things, this was that second. The overwhelming impulse that gripped them both was to obey. If Joe asked for silence, they would be tight-lipped nose-breathers until he said otherwise. The rapture that overtook them was compelling and complete. Joe offered his hand to Coyote and lifted him from the ground. If men could be changed in an instant, Nate and Coyote would be the first transformation at the hand of Blue Water. If a man could be changed in a lifetime, Nate would be the first to have witnessed it in Joe, even if Joe had missed it within himself.

Nate straightened his body, rolled his shoulders, and prepared himself to do as Joe asked. Coyote assumed his usual loose-limbed posture while shaking the blood down to the foot that showed plainly through his blown-up boot.

"Black hole," Nate said as he gripped Joe's hand soundly.

"Black hole," Joe responded in like manner.

Coyote wiggled his bare toes out of the dead remains of his boot. "Black hole, whatever that means."

"Whatever comes in doesn't get out," Nate said to Coyote.

Coyote started bouncing on his toes. "I'm with you, boys. I'm with you. I'm feelin' pretty good right now," he announced as he began to shadowbox with an imaginary foe. Slipping away from an invisible jab, he double-clutched his footwork and then ducked under a hidden right hook. "Things are really crazy, but I love crazy like a cat loves milk. Besides, I owe Blue for givin' me fresh legs and addin' a few inches to my vertical. You can count on this ol' dog. He won't be howlin' till you turn him loose." He growled as he threw a flurry of openhanded blows that would have slapped a ghost silly. Wildly baring his teeth, he howled at the new day. "Black hole, I'm in! Count on it! It's great to be alive; let's roll!" he shouted into the heavens, and they all knew this to be true.

As the three men parted ways, the change in them was more noticeable than the spring in Coyote's floppy-shoed step, and just as impossible to explain. All that used to be was no measure for all that would be coming.

"Debbie, log me out," Joe spoke softly into his radio.

"I have one additional report for today's record," Dispatcher Marshall answered, surprised by his informal address. "The village sign has just been vandalized."

"How is that possible? We don't have vandals in Toussaint, and the sign is within an eyeball's view of the station."

"I'm sorry, Chief, but the report is true. I have seen it myself."

"How bad is it?"

"It's not bad at all, Chief. In fact, the lettering is better than the original. It's just three gold-colored words that were added to the message."

"What are the words, Debbie?"

"Beneath 'In God We Trust,' someone has written 'God is Coming.'"

"Is that it? The sign is not damaged or altered in any other way?"

"Affirmative, Chief, that's it. That's the only change. The sign now says 'God is Coming.'"

Joe looked through his windshield and noticed the brittle remains of a dead grasshopper that was trapped beneath the black rubber of his wiper blade. He switched the wipers on, smearing the bug in a milky haze across the cloudy glass.

"We will let it go for now. Keep it off the air. Log me out," he said as he watched the insect reduced to a vague smudge of what it used to be.

"You're logged out, Chief. The time is zero seven hundred three."

"That doesn't sound like the chief," the day-shift dispatcher said while pouring fresh coffee into Debbie Marshall's stained cup.

"What do you mean?" Debbie asked, backing away from the microphone, but she didn't need an answer.

Joe was more feeling than thought as he drove back to his marshland home. He arrived by habit and entered through the back door, leaving his official shoes on the grass mat alongside his work boots and running shoes. He hung his keys on the old horseshoe nail that had been hammered into the doorframe more than one hundred years before, and then walked directly into his closed bedroom, locked in the pattern of his ways. He removed his hat, gun belt, and gold shield and placed them in order on a closed chest that was next to his bed. All other pocket items were placed neatly on the windowsill. Then he removed his official uniform, piece by piece, and hung it on individual wooden hangers in his mostly empty closet. He walked into the bathroom, removed his socks, and placed them on the towel rack next to the sink. He brushed his teeth without catching his image in the mirror before taking a long, hot shower that turned his skin red. After toweling himself dry, he looked at his reflection, passed inspection, and then fell into his bed. Sleep came quickly, without the troubled labor of a tossing mind. Had this been an ordinary day, Joe would have remained awake for another five hours, following through on daily tasks that had clear-cut endings. He liked order in his life. When things were out of place, he had to sleep.

Nate followed Joe's request to go directly home. He called his command officer, asked politely for a three-day leave, which was granted, and then prepared the eleven spices of the ketoret incense for burning. The burning of the ketoret was a ritual that was said to not only smell like God, but the formula itself came directly from God. Unlike the earthy smell and curling cloud of the white sage, and the sweetgrass smudge sticks of his native offerings, the ketoret released a fragrant bouquet of smoke that rose straight as a pole and persuaded the senses to believe that God was closer than a prayer. On this day, Nate believed that the ketoret was the way to go. With the spices properly mixed, he lit a brass oil lamp, and then, holding the ketoret in the palms of both hands, he slowly released the compound over the flame until every particle of it was burned. Satisfied with his good and true offering of the elements, he picked up his Bible and began praying while pacing the floor.

Nate's home was a collection of every step that he had taken in his life. Surrounded by hundreds of framed reminders of his past, a holy collage of sentimental favors suspended in time with the glorious moment, he saved everything, each wall a reminder of who he had been and who he wanted to become. Newspaper stories, photographs, athletic medals, and civic awards were mounted with care and hung with respect for the helpers who made such things possible. Enclosed in this shrine of what a man could make of his life with heaven's blessing and human hands, Nate felt loved by God. When he was quarterbacking for the Volunteers and the sports writers interviewed him after the games, he faithfully gave credit for his performance to "*God, to the team, and to the fierce hitting of Blue Water.*" When he moved on to other challenges, those of easy nature and those that sustained life on the thinnest breath, he always thanked God first for all good things and then even the bad, if they made him better. Nate was thankful for just about everyone and everything that came his way, great or small. It was all worth remembering. As he paced and prayed within these walls of comfort, he was certain that what he had witnessed in Blue Water's touch was only the beginning of the greatest memory of his lifetime, but the end was not far away.

Just like Nate and every other good man in Toussaint, Coyote listened well when Joe Water spoke. Even though he was filled to bursting with everything that he would like to spill at Violet's, he went home to wait on further word. He lived within the razor wire enclosure known as the boneyard, where wheeled steel came to rest when it could no longer roll. His home was a small concrete block structure that only a man of Coyote's sensibilities could love. Painted green with a low-pitched red metal roof, it suited the graveyard look of the place where steel corpses were buried uniformly on top of each other in crumpled ruin. At the back of the yard, standing a story above the tallest heap of rusted yesterday, was his statement about what he could still do today; he called it the gridiron. Built on the same dimensions as a football field, the 160-by-360-foot steel building provided a nice spread for doing his best work. The wide-open layout gave him the elbow room to juke his way between hand tools like a country doctor, diagnosing and then repairing every wounded vehicle by touching and listening to their symptoms. His skills for getting them back on the road were supernatural compared to other mechanics who couldn't solve a problem without an engine analyzer and an advanced degree. The vast concrete floor was clean, with no visible clue of any lost fluids from dripping gaskets or ruptured lines, and the tools of his trade shined beneath the silver light that burned a steady drain on Toussaint's power grid. Protected by a small pack of coon-chasing hounds that were just as content with treeing a man, Coyote's boneyard contained most of what he wanted, but less than what he needed.

He drove his pickup through the front gate, chained the fence behind him, and then headed directly for the gridiron. He took the last six-pack of beer out of the old Frigidaire that was airbrushed with flames in the school colors, opened one longneck with the church key on his leather fob, and then started working on Hillary's wounded condition. It was what he wanted to do, what he felt that he needed to do, what he had to do. He would work until he tapped the last drop of cold brew into his system. When that time came, he could handle other things. When that time came, he might think better on the particulars of what he had experienced; it wouldn't take long.

Violet Love descended the back staircase that joined her private world with her life as the purveyor of common sense in all matters between men and women. She swayed like the pendulum on a fine old clock as she moved about the place that she inherited when she was eighteen. It was the perfect match for the charming young woman who mixed her soothing wisdom with every drink that was poured to satisfaction. It excited the men to be taught a woman's lesson by Violet as the liquor warmed their blood, and it comforted the women to have their men eager to show what they had learned. She was, without question, the prescribed remedy for the nagging ache that drives good men to do bad things. In the years that drew her blue jeans closer to her skin, she remained a compelling ally to any woman who wanted the best from her man.

Violet maintained the appearance of her business as she did her own good looks: tight, clean, and perfumed. The bar had a purple neon blush, with the scent of burned tobacco smoke and alcohol the preferred fragrance. Violet's Friendly Tavern was the living room of Toussaint's self-expression. When citizens stopped in for a drink or a comforting word, they were guaranteed a warm rush of familiar things, a taste of home, flavored with a sense of belonging. It was the mortal heart of all that coursed through the village, and as such, Violet worked long hours to keep it so. She was busy doing just that when a stranger walked through the door. It spooked Violet because she did not hear the door open, nor did she hear it close behind the stranger. She just turned around from wiping down the mirror behind the bar, and there he stood, quietly watching her work as the dusty rays of morning light framed his body.

"Please excuse me for interrupting your work," he said with a deep, mellow tone.

"It's too late for that. The deed is done. How did you get in here?"

"Through the doorway," he answered without moving from the spot where he stood.

"That door should have been locked."

"It was open for me, and there were no hours posted outside, so I just came in to see what you had to offer."

"Everyone knows the days and the hours of operation," she said, sizing him up with her eyes wide open, knowing how to stall a man. "You're early. Today is Sunday, and I don't open until two hours before the first church bell tolls. We don't do a paid business on the Lord's Day, but as long as you're here and I have a full bar, what would you like?"

"I would like you to not be afraid."

Violet inched carefully toward the nickel-plated revolver that was kept beneath the bar. "Do I have a reason to be afraid?"

"Certainly not, what chance would I have against a woman like you on the Lord's Day?"

"No chance at all," she said as her right hand rested confidently on the gun.

"No doubt," he agreed while standing motionless. "My work is done today. I just wanted some refreshment before moving on."

Confident in her judgment of men and her marksmanship at close range, both of which had improved hundredfold since the day Joe Water laid to rest the three men who trespassed on her womanhood, strangers would forever be scrutinized with her thumb close to the hammer. "Let me get a closer look at you."

He did not twitch nerve or muscle. "Is it safe?"

Securing her trigger finger in the ready-to-fire position, she waved him forward with her left hand. "Step up to the bar, and I'll let you know."

As the man moved toward Violet, she was struck by the handsome cut of his face, the soundless fall of his feet on the floor, and the fresh, sweetened smell of the air that surrounded him. He was unlike any other man that she had ever laid eyes on. His beauty stared back at her; his manner completely disarmed her.

"May I sit?" he asked politely.

She could not refuse. She relaxed her grip on the revolver and then placed both of her hands in front of her on the bar top. "Only if you behave."

"That's all that I ever do."

"Then sit and I'll pour you one welcoming drink, compliments of the house." She was taken by his look and warmed by his presence. She felt the same familiar flush that Joe Water aroused in her, on those rare days when he sat on that same stool and ordered coffee. Between long draws of the black brew, Joe would sit with his left elbow on the bar top with his thumb stroking his chin, holding thoughts that never reached expression. He rarely spoke except to thank her for her service or return a greeting from a neighbor. Violet wondered if this unfamiliar man would favor Joe's behavior or have something on his mind to say. Without asking for his preference, she poured twenty-year-old bourbon into a rocks glass and then placed it in front of him.

"Will this do?"

"Indeed," he answered, sweeping the drink beneath his nose to savor the aged quality of its vapors.

Violet kept her attention fixed on his movements. She was caught up in every detail of his manner and unaware that she was staring at him as he sniffed the rare quality of the bourbon.

He swirled the drink into a compact whirlpool within the glass. "This spirit has character. It speaks quietly but carries sufficient power to command your thoughts."

Violet continued to stare, watching the rhythmic twisting of glass and hand.

"God is the provider of wine that makes the heart of mortal men rejoice," he said, holding the spiraling evidence up to the light.

"That's not wine," Violet cautioned, finding a reason to address him.

"Agreed, this is much better." Then he poured the proof down his throat in a single swallow and then placed the empty glass on the bar top. "Thank God also for that which is not wine."

"Would you like another?"

"No, I will remember this one drink for a long time. There must be temperance in all things, or we will surely find our way to hell."

"You are a Christian man?" she announced, more declaration than question.

"I have my faith," he answered with the sweet aroma of his breath mingling with the barrel-flavored whiskey.

"But you quote scripture from the Bible like you have studied every word."

"I have learned many things during my time, and the most important thing that I have learned is still waiting for expression."

Violet inhaled the flavor that rose from his body. She was taken in by every nuance of this man, every hint that he was special, and every tone that provoked her to wonder about those things that were most important to a single woman in Toussaint.

"Are you a God-fearing man?"

"No, I am God-friendly," he said with a million-mile stare that outdistanced every thought that she had ever known.

"What does that mean? Do you believe in God or not?"

"Are the rest of your citizens as confident in their judgment as you? Does the collective wisdom of this place conclude that one must fear God in order to know him?"

"It's just an expression."

"An expression of what?"

"An expression of respect, I guess."

"That really is an interesting notion. It explains much more about you than you probably realize."

"I'm sorry if I offended you, but this is a Christian village, and I was just wondering if you felt the same way." Violet shook as an anxious chill rolled over her flesh.

"I saw the village sign, and it speaks to me." He motioned to himself with an open hand held against his heart.

"Well that's good, then. In God you trust. You have answered my question." She felt the curious pleasure of his eyes upon her.

"No, the sign says much more than that. It also says that God is coming."

"Not so, not unless the sign has changed since I woke up," Violet said, breathing in the blended aromas that were filling her senses. "I know every detail of that sign, and there is no such message anywhere, no way, no how."

"It is there."

"Are you lying?" She laughed, still yielding to the sentiment that so splendid a man should not be provoked.

"Again you judge me. Is there no end to your authority?" he said with a clear but gentle sarcasm.

"I'm sorry, but that, too, is really just an expression."

"I thought so. Do you ever mean what you say?"

Violet had never been caught in a trap of her own design before this stranger arrived. Conversation was usually an exchange of words that took place to fill up the time between friends of common thought. She was never pressed to think that the same words could mean different things to a man like this, but the trap was sprung, and the feeling was exciting.

"Walk down the street and see for yourself, Violet, and then you might see for others."

"When I'm done here. This woman's work is never finished."

"You and God have a lot in common."

"Is that an expression?" she said, thinking that this time she caught him in a trap of words.

"No, that is the truth. You both have a lot of work to do."

"Ain't that a fact." She blushed from the compliment and the nervous heat that was rising from her body. "You are a very different kind of man."

"Yes, I am, Violet." He looked around the room as if to find someone to agree. "Yes, I am."

Violet wanted to touch this man. She could not resist the urge to reach across the bar and feel his flesh. Pats on the back, a stroke on the arm, a squeeze of the hand were all familiar gestures of her sincerity. In her many years behind the bar, she always used that which served her customers best, but this time, the scratching was meant to satisfy her own itch. As she moved to place her hand on top of his, he looked straight into her and smiled.

"Thank you," he said.

It stopped her cold, within a heartbeat of her desire.

"Behold, I will send you Elijah the prophet before the coming of the great and dreadful day of the Lord."

The startling words that issued forth from him rang into her ears as if from some distant place. She was certain that he had spoken them, but like his arrival, she was spooked by the unexpected nature of the experience. "What…What did you say?" was all she could manage in return.

"I will see you again, Violet. I must be going now." He stood up and walked toward the door in an effortless manner that seemed discordant with the powerful build of his body.

Violet shook her head in the wind of his scented trail, bewildered by the quick turn of events and the uncertain meaning of what she had heard. "What? What did you say?"

"Read the sign." He said nothing more and then closed the door behind him.

Violet reached for the bottle of bourbon. She poured a double shot to inspire her memory. It went down like juice in the morning. She poured another, a charity shot. Until today, it was the kind of drink that she never served on Sunday. No one laid money on her bar on Sunday. On Sunday she was charitable, just like she had been with the exotic crash victim on Friday. Sunday was a freewill offering, and she just gave it away free—and she was helping herself freely as well. The second round went down harder. She swallowed the stinging taste of it and then collapsed on her stool behind the bar. As good as it was, the pride of Kentucky did not go well on an empty stomach.

The insistent noise of Joe's telephone demanded his attention. With or without sleep, when his phone called, he listened. He arose from his bed and walked naked through the house, disturbed but unashamed. Picking the phone up, he cleared his voice and then spoke into the receiver with as much clarity as a sleep-deprived man could muster.

"Yes?"

"Chief, you better come uptown." The rookie dispatcher's voice cracked with alarm.

"Why?"

"A crowd has gathered at the edge of the village. Traffic has stopped dead. This will impact the whole county if we don't move these citizens out of here!"

"Calm down, son. Tell the sergeant to just give the order, and they will move."

"I don't think so, Chief. They won't listen to anyone but you."

"What are they doing in the street?"

"They're having a prayer meeting, Chief."

"A prayer meeting?"

"Yes, sir, a prayer meeting. I can't explain it, but you really have to come up here and get a personal grip on this situation."

"Are these our citizens? Do they belong to us?"

"Yes, sir, they are, and they do, and you really need to move them out before things get ugly!"

"Affirmative, call everyone up."

"Everyone's up here but you, Chief."

"Affirmative, I'm on my way."

Joe Water was heading into his third day of disruption. There was no end to what had begun on Friday night. All that he had known and served was being swallowed into this timeless anomaly that he did not understand and, worse, he had no way to control. He could not recover without sleep, and it was always the comfort of sleep that carried him from one end to the other of his episodic life. When he finished a job, it was complete, tidy, and wrapped up with a definite sunset. When he closed the book, it stayed closed, but he could not close the book on this one. It kept opening up on him with new chapters being written by an unseen, but often heard, author whom he neither recognized nor believed in.

Chapter 6

Joe Water sped south on Route Nineteen with the stick resting on the seat beside him. He seldom removed the branch from its revered spot in his home, but when he did, it served as his third eye, a reminder to keep all things in perspective. He was who he was, the chief officer of the peace. In a rowdy crowd of outsiders, he did not want to be less.

By the time he crossed the tracks, he could see for himself the cause of the dispatcher's dismay. Toussaint was under siege by a slow tangle of cars jammed into tight locations in the streets or scattered in bad angles across front yards and alleyways. The noise and clutter of people and traffic sprawled across every surface was uncommon and unwanted. All traffic was at a dead stop, and it was Joe's job to get it moving again. He hit his lights and siren to warn them that he was coming to open the roads and, if need be, their minds.

"Dispatcher, this is Water. Where are my units placed?"

"I'm sorry, Chief, but I can't locate any of them."

"Repeat!"

"I can't locate any of them."

"Dispatcher, explain your problem."

"They are all out of their vehicles and in the crowd, and they have broken communication."

"Log me in!"

"Will do, Chief, the time is ten hundred one."

"I copy that."

"Roger that, Chief; go get 'em, buddy," the dispatcher said, comforted by the secure feeling that Joe Water was now in command.

Joe would have corrected the dispatcher's break from formality, but he had a bigger cat to skin than the one behind the desk. He maneuvered his cruiser through the muddled knot of vehicles and pedestrians until he reached the corner of State Route Nineteen and Water Street. He stopped in the middle of the intersection, exited his vehicle with a handful of road flares, and then commandeered three passing truckers to direct traffic. Joe was the best at sizing up men with leadership abilities; he picked these three for their imposing look and confident manner. Within moments he had the three truckers organized and educated in his method of moving bodies.

"Hey you!" the burly truckers commanded while pointing hot flares at startled motorists. "Keep moving!"

They ordered with such intensity and clarity of purpose that each driver who was still in a vehicle had little choice but to conform. It didn't take long for the three men to manage the east end of the village. Having confidence in their abilities to maintain control, Joe left the three men and then worked his way up the street on foot.

The west end of the village was a stalemate. In the middle of the block, the noisy clamor of the outsiders who were pushing their indignation up Water Street was halted by the resolve of Toussaint's citizens. Standing shoulder to shoulder, with their backs against the snarl of hot-tempered traffic, the Sunday army of villagers did not budge amidst the riotous jeers of the outsiders to do so. It was a strange scene to behold, even for those who had worldly experiences of other-end-of-scale behaviors. Even for those who had passed this way before, through the limiting streets of Toussaint, it was still an extreme set of conditions, human or otherwise.

Joe stepped easily through the crowd of outsiders who had left their vehicles to confront the source of their frustration. He was straightforward and compelling with his word of choice.

"Move," he commanded, and they obeyed. Man for man, woman for woman, they did not stand in his way. When he reached the impassable gathering presented by his people, it only took a hard look from his blue eye to give him room to pass. The Volunteers parted and then quickly closed ranks behind him, allowing only Joe to receive a clear path to the object of their devotion. As he drew nearer to the site, he counted the entire fleet of village cruisers parked bumper to bumper, surrounding the village sign. The lawmen were out of their vehicles but near enough to respond to their radios; they just failed to do so. The smoking letters "GOD IS COMING" had them transfixed, much like everyone else who was pressing for a look. The writing stood out bolder and more perfectly formed than any other letters on the village sign. Each golden letter was smoldering from some hidden fire and gripped the attention of everyone except the chief officer of the peace.

"Answer the call," he said, but they did not respond.

"Now!" he shouted, breaking the spell that the simmering letters held over them.

"What should we do?" the sergeant asked.

"Do your job!"

"Sure, Chief, but it's not clear what our job is? The sign has everyone transfixed, and it's not right to bust up a prayer meeting."

"Improvise! Do you need a training manual for every situation? Prayer meeting or not, your job requires you to keep the peace. Are you able? I gave you rank because you swore that you were able. I believed you then. Do you believe in yourself now? Are you able?" Joe's attention was on the sergeant, but his words were loud and meant for all of his men.

"Yes, Chief, I am able."

"Then get busy! All of you get busy and send these people home. Now!"

Only Joe could give an order that everybody understood and obeyed without contempt. Even in the light of the burning sign, his words carried more authority than what their eyes were witnessing. With no further encouragement needed, all of his officers returned to their patrol cars, answered the dispatcher's call, and then went back to work, just like any other day on the job. When he was satisfied that his men were on task, he turned his attention to the volunteer firemen who stood with their limp hoses in hand.

"Put it out," Joe said.

"We can't," they answered in a bewildered chorus.

"We've poured more water on those words than we doused on the homecoming bonfire, and they just keep smoking," the fire captain said. "As far as I can tell, it's not even burning. It goes against nature and everything I've learned since I've worn the captain's hat. I don't understand it, and I don't think the rest of the village understands it. It's a sign, all right, and it's too powerful to ignore. What do you think, Blue? Do you know what's happening here? Is it a miracle?"

Joe surveyed the hushed crowd. They were looking to him for an answer, and he was probing the scene to provide one. With both eyes scanning the anxious assembly, he fixed his sights on a potent-looking stranger who stood out like a man who was hiding the secret to the moiling message.

"Come here," Joe said, expecting the man to reveal some gesture of guilt, and true to Joe's instinct about men with something to hide, the man greeted his attention with a clever smile, confirming to Joe that he had found his mark.

The stranger stepped forward, moving through the tightly packed mob with a smooth and easy motion. Joe sized him up with each advancing step and recognized without a doubt that this man was different, the sort of different that could upset the balance of things with just the slightest tip. As he drew closer to Joe, the air took on an uncommon sweetness, fresher than lilac, more pleasing than rose. It was the same enigmatic aroma that attended every inconsistent event that had flowed unreal since Friday.

"Relax, Joseph, there is no need for you to be troubled," the imposing stranger said as he closed in on Joe.

"Stand down," Joe answered, bracing himself for any number of nameless things that this powerful stranger could deliver.

The stranger moved closer, gliding without effort, to meet Joe.

"Fair warning," Joe cautioned, shifting his weight to his right hip.

The stranger took his last step out of range of Joe's left foot. "Read the sign, be still, and listen."

It was the voice that had called to Joe in the night, the voice that knew his name. The sound of it was unforgettable, and now that it stood before him, Joe did the only thing he could do to keep the peace.

"You're under arrest," he said.

"Some men are more than they believe. Some men are more than they understand. Which manner of man are you, Joseph?"

"I am the manner of man who is arresting you," Joe said abruptly, fixing both of his eyes on the stranger's unyielding stare.

"Can you make such a judgment just by looking at me?"

"I can."

"Are you certain?"

"I am," Joe said loud enough to be heard by those who were listening.

The stranger was unimpressed. "It is good to be clear and certain when such judgment can change so many things in a life."

Joe was steady on his feet, balanced of mind and body. "Be advised, as the chief officer of the peace, I have the authority to make such a decision."

"You have the authority only as long as your judgment is clear."

"Clear as a bell. Are you going to talk me to death, or are you going to cooperate?"

"You know yourself, and you know your job. So do I. Therefore, I fully and completely cooperate with the chief officer of the peace. With all of these good people as my witnesses, I surrender myself to your authority."

Joe relaxed; he took the stranger at his word, and he believed his word to be good. He could be sure about such things when his gut feeling was stronger than the circumstantial evidence placed before him.

"Do not move from this spot," Joe said, allowing the stranger to stand unrestrained at his side. As expected, the visitor did exactly as Joe had ordered; standing powerfully erect and perfectly still, he stirred not and said no more.

As the letters continued to meld into the sign behind him, Joe Blue Water finally gave the village what it wanted to hear. "Clear the street. Go home. I have everything in hand, and when I find the answer, I will tell you."

It wasn't much to hear, but coming from Joe, it was enough to move them. He scanned the crowd for any dissenters, but there were none to be found. He listened for a voice to challenge his authority, but none was raised. Even during times like this, when men's faith was encouraged by their vision, Joe Water still had the last word between the confluence of the Toussaint and Portage Rivers. They believed in him because his word never failed them, and surely it would not fail them today. On this day of revelation, when he spoke, the people of Toussaint listened. He had everything in hand…and they believed him.

"Okay, Joe…"

"No sweat, Blue…"

"Whatever you say, Chief…"

"Everybody over to Violet's!"

They moved with obedient hearts and thirsty souls. It was a common condition that could only be quenched at Violet's Friendly Tavern before kneeling in church. They stayed together, they moved together, the peace was kept, and by the time they left the bar, they were pretty sure about what they had seen. During church they sang and prayed with a zealous spirit that was tuned for this occasion. There was only song and prayer; there would be no sermon on this day.

With the streets opened, the outsiders who had been trying to push through the crowd were now able to view the sign. Some took photographs, some laughed, some were moved to tears, some wanted to believe, some rejected every notion of belief, but none stayed long enough to witness anything beyond the smoking sign. They were not Toussaint folk, and it didn't take them long to walk away with their mouths opened wide to tell the world. Joe stood his ground until the last of them dispersed and the clamor was reduced to a normal hum. As the sign continued to smoke, Joe turned his full attention to the stranger.

"How do we put it out?" Joe asked, convinced that the sign burned by some trick of the stranger's hand.

"You cannot extinguish such a thought."

"How long will it burn?"

"I cannot answer that."

"What if I break your arm?"

"You can try."

Joe was afflicted with three days of festering doubt in a life that was medicated with universal order. He arrived at the only conclusion that he could make, given the conditions that were stretching him thin.

"Follow me. I don't buy what you're selling."

As the two of them walked east to where his cruiser was parked, the chief officer of the peace felt like squaring off with this man who had upset his world. There were days when he would have done so, days when a fight could easily satisfy his soul, days when victory brought a conclusion, but this was the end of such days. There could be no stopping of what this stranger delivered, no easy solutions to apply. Joe couldn't rely on muscle and grit to halt the approaching test of his authority to keep the peace; he could slow it down some, but it would definitely arrive.

Joe's cruiser remained in its fixed position in the middle of the intersection. The three truckers who moved the traffic on the east end of the village were still on the job, dutifully answering their appointment to assist. Their skill at getting people to listen was so good that Joe's parked cruiser was no challenge for them to work around. With the flow of traffic under control, Joe thanked each of them for guiding travelers through Toussaint. He offered many things in appreciation for their time and service: a handshake, a meal, a tank of diesel fuel from the village pump, and an official commendation that would be mailed to them from the village. They took only the handshake. Joe was grateful for such men. They were the kind of men who he liked to fish with on Lake Erie, the kind who picked their lures by the time of day and packed their own lunches for work. There was no mystery to such men, no hidden intent to their words or actions. They were what they were, unlike the stranger who sat in the back of his cruiser; he was something else. Instead of holding the stranger in a cell at the station, Joe set out for Twin Bridges to uncover what more this man could be.

"Dispatcher, this is Water. I'm traveling north on Route Nineteen. Over!"

"Affirmative, Chief, the time is thirteen hundred one. Are you going to book the suspect? Over!"

"Negative, but I am going to escort him out of town. Over!"

"Do you have a copy of his vehicle registration and license? Maybe we should run his prints to see if he has any priors? Are you ten-four on releasing him? Over!"

"Hold on," Joe answered the dispatcher without signing off the air, and then he turned his microphone off. Studying the stranger's reflection in the mirror, Joe saw the same sly smile that spoke louder than words. He brought the cruiser to a slow stop in the middle of the northbound lane; the stranger continued to smile, serene and unafraid. Joe turned his head to the untroubled man in the backseat.

"Hold your hands up, palms facing me," he said.

The stranger obliged, revealing the smoothness of his skin that had neither wrinkle, nor line, nor any identifying feature that was common to men. He continued to smile, and then he winked at Joe, the kind of wink that confirms a shared confidence. Joe did not endorse the notion; he just turned back to his radio, convinced that he was making the right call.

"Affirmative, we won't be holding him. Over!"

"Confirmed," the dispatcher answered.

Joe reached for the branch and held it tightly in his right hand and then traveled on toward his destination. He looked in his mirror and saw the reflection of the smiling man who continued to hold his palms up for inspection. They both remained silent until Joe turned the cruiser into the stones at Twin Bridges.

"You can put your hands down. I get the difference," he said without looking back.

"Thank you," the stranger replied.

Had Joe been looking, he would have noticed that the man's smile was broader, more satisfied than clever, but it didn't matter; the obvious was no longer circumstantial. It was what it was, and Joe wanted it to go away. He exited the cruiser and then opened the rear door. "Follow me," he said.

They walked out to the point where Joe had first experienced the redolent being beside him. There was no reason for him to deny that this was the voice in the dark. His scent was so memorable, so familiar that it made an imperishable trail back to its possessor. It wouldn't take a bloodhound to find him; the smell marked him and screamed out his presence.

"You were here last Friday night," Joe stated plainly, letting the stranger know that he was not confused on that fact.

"Yes."

"Did you save my life?"

"Your life is not mine to save."

"Can't we just talk plainly here? I'll ask a question, and you answer it. You can stop spinning the words around. I'm getting tired of chasing down your meanings." Joe focused his blue eye on the stranger. "Did you, in fact, save my life?"

"No, I have no control over who lives or dies. I just do what I'm sent to do, nothing more, and nothing less."

"You just do what you're sent to do? Who would send you to Toussaint?"

"If I told you, would you even believe me? Do you think that you're prepared to know, Joseph, given that you live in the assurance of the natural world?"

"Just tell me, buddy. The suspense is killing me!" Joe shouted, reaching his limits of civility.

"God sent me."

"God sent you. Whose God would that be?"

"There is only one Creator, Joseph. Your people call him God, so I will use it as a point of reference. He has been called many things throughout the time of man, sometimes nothing at all. In words that you will appreciate, Joseph, he is what he is."

"He is what he is," Joe repeated, welcoming the completeness of the thought.

"That is the essence of God, Joseph. He is what he is. He is real, as real as that branch of the Methuselah tree that you think so much of. I understand your enthusiasm for holding that branch so sacred, but he actually feels your cause. He is touched by every universal breath that is heaved upon him, seasoned by a length of time that you cannot imagine. The Methuselah tree is old, Joseph, but God is eternal."

Joe listened to what the stranger had to say, but he didn't swallow all of it. He was weakened by sleep deprivation and the revelations of this unearthly being who showed his face during the most confused and chaotic moments. His world was spinning as it collapsed in on him, and he was sickened with the dizzying weight of it. He could not accept what he could not comprehend, and his confusion was a suffocating groan in his throat. So much had happened, so much had taken place that Joe Water, a man among men, was having trouble remembering how his own name had come to be.

"Are you an angel?" Joe asked, struggling to find himself.

"If that is what you want to believe. I, too, am only what I am. Call me what you like. I have more than one thousand names, and I will answer to them all, if I am called in earnest. The only thing that you have to know about me is that I am the one who has come to deliver the message to you."

"Why have you come to me? If you are what you say you are, then you know that I have no faith in spooks and ghosts and powers that hide themselves in shadows. I see you now, and I'm talking to you now, but I may not be right in my thinking. Things haven't been so clear to me lately, and you're not making it any easier to see. I'm going to need a little more than that."

"What do you need, Joseph?"

"Something more, I don't know."

"Isn't your life enough? You have it back, don't you? Trust in him completely, and never rely on what you know or what you think you know. Remember him in everything you do, and he will show you the right way. He knows your life; he knows what you have been and what you would like to be.

You have studied your own life and have resolved many things, but now you come to the point where your mind knows that it is not what it thought. Thought goes; faith remains. Take heed, Joseph, the governments of the world outside of Toussaint are ruling on a hunch, long after the facts have proven otherwise. You will understand in the days to come. Sort out the false clues and bad assumptions. You are the blood of the lamb; you will do what is right. What more is there to believe?"

"What more is there to believe? I am the blood of my father, and his father before him, and his father before him. None of them were covered in sheep's wool. What a bunch of nonsense."

"It is not nonsense; it is you, Joseph. You are the blood of the lamb, the last man standing, the Lone Man in the traditions of the Native tribes, the sole survivor."

"Finally, you say something that takes less digging than a grave. I am the last of the Water kin. That is for sure."

"You are more than that. Water is the solvent of life. Without it, life dries up and dies. Believe me, Joseph, you are more than the end of your bloodline. You are the end of his bloodline, and you must bring things back into balance. The actions of mankind demonstrate a mindless and selfish waste that will consume what he has created; what remains will circle the drain until it disappears into the dark hole from which it came."

"You're speaking my language, but I don't understand a word that you are saying," Joe complained.

"You must, and you will."

"I might if I could think straight. I'm not at my best right now. Why don't you go away and let me sleep on this? Give me some time to think it through."

"The time is now. If you sleep on this, it will end here. You will take your last breath on the side of the road, along with the rest of your kind who are asleep at the wheel; but you will not let that happen, Joseph. In spite of your human guilt, you have been a good man. You have not been deluded by desire or hostility, and you have lived without shame and followed that which is right to follow. You cannot hide yourself from him or refuse the duty that you must perform. It is your nature, it is your calling, and it is who you are."

"I'm just a man; if I were more, my father would have told me so."

"Your father is telling you now. You were more than a man long ago, Joseph, but you have taken too much time to consider it. You are what you are, we all are, and it is now time for you to do what you were put here to do."

"What was I put here to do?"

"Listen to your own words. You were put here to be the chief officer of the peace. Do your job, Joseph. Just do your job."

"I have been doing my job."

"Do it outside of town. Do it so that the world knows," the being with one thousand names said as he vanished into thin air.

Chapter 7

Joe Water walked along the banks of the Toussaint River, over the land that had borne the weight of his footprints since he was a child, when running as only a boy can run he scattered them lightly through the lost minutes of the day. Now his shoes were filled with the weight of tomorrow, he pressed them deeply, with more intent, aware that the hours were now being kept. Joe was thoughtful about time. There was the kind of time that men reserved to measure their days. He had confidence in the dependable hour, the fractional minute. To Joe this was good time, real time, and he used it well. Then there was the kind of time that was not absolute, unreal time, the stretch of transcendent moments that passed while dreaming or losing concentration, the kind of time that spun from a web where each parallel strand diverged on its own course, for its own reason. At impossible moments, through forces that could not be explained, strands could intersect, welcoming every possibility. To Joe this was bad time, deficient in rhythm, lacking reliable limits, the kind of time that lived inside a man's head and had little design except to confuse his purpose. All of the events from Friday to this moment could have crossed over this intersection of possibility. If gods and angels could move like this, then they could be what men believed them to be.

The more that Joe thought about these things, the heavier his feet fell upon the ground. He was hands-on with the world. The critical mass of his understanding congealed around his experiences. His eyes and ears were his most reliable witnesses, and if he lost confidence in their veracity, what could he believe? If his senses betrayed him, how could he hold on? How could he follow through? He had to be sure, he had to know, and he had to believe that he would figure it out even if he was shorthanded. Joe carried this heavy burden to his cruiser and then headed for town, squeezing the stick in his right hand, shaking his head, and hoping that an answer would fall out of his brain.

Sunday drinking at Violet's Friendly Tavern was a communion of red wine and sourdough pretzels. She served nothing more than this, and she never charged for the service. Beside the door was a collection plate for any freewill offering that a Sunday drinker might contribute; their generosity always paid better than a regular hour's profits. Any Sunday was a bonus payday for Violet, but today was an extraordinary day of tithing. Men and women dug deep into next week's payday to thank God for delivering the sign. In spite of Joe's words to disregard the evidence, the Toussaint faithful were feeling pretty generous about their beliefs and wondering aloud why the man who they respected most was so unmoved by the miracle. They could have asked him when he came through the door, but since Friday they were keeping all thoughts about Joe between themselves. As Joe walked up to the bar, their eyes said more than the voices that greeted him.

"Would you like a cup of coffee, Chief?" Violet asked.

"Ice water will do," he answered, standing at the bar with his back to the room.

Violet drew him the drink and stuck a straw in it knowing that he drank straight from the rim of the glass. Joe removed the straw, wiped it with a paper napkin, folded the napkin three times, and then placed both items to the right of the drink on the bar. Violet knew the routine; she was just wondering if Joe still practiced the behavior. Her polished smile told Joe that she remembered.

"Something funny?" he asked as he removed his hat by the brim and placed it on the bar.

"Nothing out of the ordinary, Blue," she said with a glib turn of her smile, "but I do have a question."

Violet was the only person other than Nate who could press Joe for details, so he took a long, left-handed pull off the rim of his glass to wet his answer. He placed the glass on the bar top as he swallowed down the finer details of her face: the curve of her mouth, the small bump on the bridge of her nose, the curl of her blonde lashes, and finally those rare eyes that were common only to her.

"I'm all yours," he said as he looked into the playful black centers of her huckleberry eyes.

Violet leaned her body into the bar. "What did you do with that fine man that you arrested?"

"What does he mean to you?"

"He was here this morning," she said, tapping a finger lightly on the edge of the bar.

"Did you serve him?" Joe asked, turning the burden of proof onto Violet.

Violet put both of her elbows onto the bar, folded her hands together, and rested her chin on top. She squeezed her right eye closed and raised her eyebrow above an open left eye as if sighting Joe down the barrel of a gun. "Yes, I did."

"Did he take communion?"

"No, he did not!"

"What did you serve him on Sunday morning, Violet?"

"I served him something that you wouldn't touch…my best bourbon."

"Is that the same poison that you poured into that woman I hauled out of the river?"

Violet lifted her head up and then patted Joe tenderly on his left cheek. "That woman," she groaned. "Poor Chief, is that the only detail that you remember? She was definitely a woman, and she was most definitely not one that you would easily forget, but poor Blue has forgotten just like the rest of us. It's a curious condition, one worth investigating."

Joe turned his head away from Violet, uneasy about more than her touch. The room was full of listeners and private talkers; it always was when Joe and Violet crossed words.

"Well that hard-to-forget-but-still-forgotten woman mixed it up a little. She started with the bourbon, and then she ended up in the arms of the Green Fairy."

"You should have kept that Fairy in the bottle. We don't serve liquor on Sunday in Toussaint," he scolded, keeping the heat on Violet.

"Were you listening? It's not like you to miss the details. He didn't drink the Fairy; he drank the bourbon. She drank both. She was serious, but for him it was just a friendly drink, and I didn't charge him. It was just a friendly offering to a friendly man. You know that I play by the rules, Blue. I always have," she answered with her maize-hued eyebrows arched flawlessly above her somber expression. "Does a magistrate's robe go with that badge? If it does, I'll find a bench for you to sit on. Do you want to listen, or do you want to judge?"

Joe did not answer. It was hard to tie up loose ends when the entire rope was frayed.

"He left after one drink," Violet said as she removed the towel from the tight rear pocket of her curve-hugging jeans. Like honey on the tip of a spoon, she sweetened whatever she was stirred into. Under the quiet stare of Joe Water, she wiped the top of the bar in slow, circular strokes that held his attention more than the words she was speaking. "I don't know which way he went, but he wasn't anywhere near that sign when it started smoking. I know because I witnessed the whole event. I left the bar to take a look at the sign because he told me that the words were there and I just had to see it for myself, so I did. I saw it, Joe, and I kept wondering how such perfect lettering managed to make the sign without a motion from the town council."

Joe followed the movement of her hand as she spoke, inhaling the flavor that he knew as Violet.

"Well I was just standing there, speculating about who gave the word to add the thought, when I got this crazy feeling inside. It wasn't a bad feeling; it was just a wild feeling that made my heart race and my body flush like I was sixteen and under a full moon. You know what I'm saying, Blue." She winked while clicking her tongue inside her mouth. "And that's when the letters started to smoke. Nobody was near it, and I can testify that it just started on its own. I made the call to the dispatcher, and the rest is history. It really was a miracle, Blue. The words appeared, and just like that, they burned without really burning." Violet paused, taking a long breath from all that she had remembered. "So I just wanted to know what you did with that man because, by my word, the only thing that he's guilty of is being different."

She winked again and then leaned over the bar, close enough for both of Joe's eyes to appreciate the tiny brown freckle between the hairs of her left eyebrow that glistened with the wash of an honest woman's sweat.

"Make no mistake," he said, loud and clear, so that everyone in the room would have an answer, "I released him. He is on his way back to where he came from."

"That's too bad. A man like that is hard to let go and even harder to forget," Violet said as she twisted the towel into a locker room knot and then snapped it against Joe's chest. He was unmoved by her playful assault.

"Forget him, Violet. If you let your imagination run with this, you will end up with nothing more than tired legs." Joe took a long look over his shoulder to witness the ambient glow in the room. It was easy for him to see it in their faces, the shining light of their faith, gleaming with self-assurance, in spite of the drab facts as Joe understood them. It did not sway his confidence in his own principles. "There is an answer to every question under the sun if you open your mind enough to find it."

"Is that really what you think, Chief?" Violet asked.

"It's more than what I think; it is what I believe," he said, leaving no doubt to what they already knew about the judgment of Joe Water. Like the stranger, he, too, was different, different in the way that commands respect, not contempt, different in the ways that make a man what he is, not what you want him to be…and different enough to have you love him for it.

Joe picked up the folded napkin from the bar and placed it in the left pocket of his service shirt. Then he lifted the half-full glass to his mouth, aware that they were all staring at him, their communal conscience plainly reflected in the mirror behind the bar. They were like every other man or woman on the earth except in their faith. They didn't just pray to God, they believed in him. They believed in such a way that canceled all doubt in their thinking. God was real, and they trusted that he would be coming. They were seeing the signs, and the signs were pointing to Toussaint, and they were working on his arrival with every confident swallow of Violet's Sunday communion. Joe thought that such faith should be rewarded; such faith should wipe the slate clean of any fault that a man had by being mortal. It was good to be confident; better to be sure. Joe thought that such guarantees of belief should be written on what they experienced through life, not on their mind's eye of imagined events. From where he stood, he was looking at what they couldn't even see. It was clear to him in the mirror that their vision just didn't reach that far.

"Every curious son and daughter of God and Satan alike will show up on our doorstep to take a look at our sign, so we have to get rid of it."

"It can't be moved, Blue. You can't even put the fire out, so how could you move it?" Violet said as she leaned so close to Joe that he reached for his glass in order to put something between them. "Let it go, Blue. Whatever comes is supposed to be here."

Joe picked up his glass and then swallowed the remainder of his drink before crushing the vessel to dust in his hand. "You won't like what they bring." Then he shook the powdered bits of glass onto the bar top.

"It's okay, Blue," Violet said, and the other voices in the room agreed.

"Yeah, Blue, it's okay."

"No worries, Blue."

"No sweat, Joe."

"Let it go, Blue."

The rustle of polite concern continued to fall throughout the room, filling the empty space that separated Joe from his people. He turned and faced them, and gave them one more thing that he knew for sure.

"Toussaint will change forever," he said, and then he walked out the door with his hat in his hand.

All of Toussaint loved Joe Water, but on days like this, he was better left alone. On days like this, it made more sense to talk about him rather than talk to him, even if he was willing to listen. Nobody wanted to test his blue eye; nobody wanted to stir the tempest that brewed within the man. They were safe at Violet's with their red wine, their sourdough pretzels, and their thoughts. They never really understood him anyway, especially when he was carrying his hat.

Joe's alleged inheritance was one that he found no comfort in. He believed in making his own way, and it troubled him to think otherwise. Patrolling west toward where the sign still smoldered, the presumption that he was the pick of some other dog's litter was not sitting well with him. He still had time to think it through, but the time was shrinking, getting smaller with the hour. As he proceeded down Water Street, he saw the figure of a woman who would squeeze the moment even more. It was the woman from Friday night undulating beneath the sheer cling of her blouse, high-heeled, and practiced in the provocative stir of her movement. Her walk was enough to jerk any man's hazy recollection into absolute recognition. Joe pulled his cruiser to the curb to confirm his memory.

She opened the passenger side door without an invitation. One naked leg followed the other until she had stirred her whole being into a relaxed pose beside him.

"Hello, Chief," she whispered with a perfumed redolence that caressed each word, "are you going my way?"

Enclosed within this small space with the aphrodisiac smack of her intent filling his senses, Joe cracked his window halfway down to relieve the pressure. With the fresh Sunday breeze on the back of his neck, he inhaled every detail of the look, sound, and smell of her, not because she was so desirable, but because if she disappeared again, he wanted to make her memorable. He wanted to personalize these spirits, pull them out of the collective unconscious and name them if he could.

"Who are you?" he asked.

"It does not matter," she answered with the woozy charm of exotic spices flavoring each word.

"It matters, sister, or you wouldn't be here. Once more, who are you, and what is your relationship to the all-knowing bogey that lit up our sign?"

"I am the proof."

Joe hunched himself up higher in his seat. "You are the proof of what?"

"I am the touchstone of your humanity, the measure of your manhood."

"We won't be measuring anything, sweetheart."

"Time will tell. Start counting the days, Chief, because you only have, the days of knowing, left in your account."

"I only have, the days of knowing, left in my account? What are you, some credit card hustler? I'm not afraid of your spooky timekeeping. The days of knowing…watch out…boo!" Joe shouted out, causing the dark centers of her eyes to dilate and then squeeze down into small, concentrative circles.

"Because you cannot hold the whole universe in your head does not mean that it has no limits," she said, crossing her legs, tightening her grip on his attention.

The sound of her skin on the seat squealed with a head-thumping invitation, but Joe was not accepting it. "Because you have something to say doesn't make it worth knowing."

"Forget what you know. Forget what you think you know about who you know. You do not know enough," she said, shifting her hips closer to Joe.

Joe was economical with his language. He liked to weigh each word to give it the necessary steadiness when delivered. Even in his troubled state, sitting next to this ethereal woman, he considered all that she said before answering. He wanted to let her know that he was more than what she took him for, but she already knew.

"If a man knows every side of one thing and knows it better than anyone else, then he has a jump start on his reason for living. I know Toussaint, and that is enough for me. I was hired to keep the peace, and I will do my job," he said confidently.

"Keep the peace. Do you really believe that one man can keep the peace?" She crossed and then uncrossed her legs, flaunting the supple flesh above her knees.

Joe breathed in the sweet aroma of the glistening dew that collected on her skin. He turned his head away from the spectacle and steeled himself against the dizzying assault on his senses. "Try me."

"Love to." She swept her left arm around his shoulders, drawing her lithe body tightly against him. "Joseph, I can see that you are a man, just like any other man," she confided in low tones that fell as a warm mist along the side of his neck, "but you have an unwelcoming energy that keeps us from being close to you."

"Why would I want to be close to you?"

"Why wouldn't you, Joseph? Am I not the thing of your dreams?" She nudged the Methuselah stick against his leg with her knee. "You need us, and we need you. It is a perfect union of needful souls."

"Trouble travels in pairs. How much trouble is traveling with you?"

"More than this earth could bear witness to." She stroked her weightless hand down his arm until it came to rest on the rough surface of the stick.

"Just read the script, dark angel. You are legion. You are a multitude," Joe said, feeling the flush rise to the surface of his skin.

"Ohhhhh, Joseph, have you been reading from your little book?"

"You have me confused with someone else."

"I am not confused, Joseph. Let me inform you." She gripped the stick firmly in her right hand, lifted it into the air, and waved it in front of Joe, taunting him with his own spiritual habits. "You worship this leftover artifact like it holds the secret to your being, Joseph, but we both know that sticks have no life force once they are broken from the tree."

"Don't touch that," Joe shouted, and then he grabbed for the stick, but she was quicker and swept it out of his reach.

"You are broken from the tree, Joseph. Do you want to try again?" She continued her insult by wiggling the stick in front of his face, but Joe did not react. He was like thunder to her lightning, and he didn't need a second trial.

"Aw, don't take it so hard, Joseph. I own this game. How about if I just put it right here so it can protect you from me?" She laughed while placing the stick in his lap. "Why do you worship this old thing anyway? Do you really believe that it has the power to teach you something? Many hands before you have touched that old stick without learning anything. They died and turned to dust, and were scattered by the thousand winds that carry the dead to places you have never seen. Learn something from me, Joseph; I will be your teacher. Study me. I am not the quick and the dead. I am the alive and the willing."

Joe's heart pounded his blood into his skin, turning his face a heated red. "I'm not interested."

"Sure you are, Joseph. I can feel your authority, the potent muscularity of it. It is real and powerfully connected, just like we could be if you just let it go.

Touch me, Joseph, and tell me what you feel. Let yourself go to where a good man really belongs."

She swayed as she spoke; her movement on the seat was a tantalizing sigh of impatient flesh, a smooth proposition for a careless soul. The sound of it amplified the hum of blood rushing over his eardrums. He was trying to understand, trying to give her a reasonable life that had meaning apart from superstition and myth, but before he could sort out his thinking, she grabbed his head and gripped it with a jolting urgency, pulling his face to within inches of her mouth. Her strength was bold and ridiculously appealing. Joe Water was trembling, and it was new to him. The mind-numbing sensation of all that she was took hold of him and would not let go as her words rustled softly into his ear.

"I am here to tell you that the messenger has come. He will confide in you and mesmerize you with words and deeds that resonate with your way of life. He will not touch you as I am touching you, and even if he did, you would not feel the way that you now feel with me. He will leave you with a choice to make, a burden that will tax every reasonable thought that you could ever trust. He will insist that you believe that most of the people on this earth are creating chaos out of order and reaching beyond your bounds to the space where he dwells. To him, their noise is unbearable, and they will be pronounced as the walking dead, alive but waiting to be buried. Some of them were born into it, while others earned it on their own, but their circumstances will not matter. His judgment has no mercy. They will all go with the thousand winds because they have lost their faith, and without faith, he cannot live. Without him, your world has nothing to live for. Do you understand what I am telling you?"

"No," he answered weakly, straining to take command of his own thoughts, but the taste of her words and the dizzying rush of blood coursing through his body diluted his resolve.

"Yes, you do, Joseph, and you are the only one who can decide. Only you can make the choice between what all people are and what they will become. It is all set into motion with no hope that you can stop it from coming. They will come to you; you are the one. After you, there are no others. If you fail, he will take away all of the energy, dark and light, from this source of universal pain. You are the only one, Joseph; it is only you who can decide. You must use the time that is given to you to prepare yourself for the question."

Joe was light-headed and unsteady. A sickness collected within his throat in an urgent bubble of spit and gastric distress. He tried to break away, but her hold on him was more than the clutch of her hands. She had the power of the unknown and the forbidden, and she squeezed him like a lemon. Trembling and quivering, exhausted from the flux of random thoughts that flashed and sparked in his brain, Joe could only manage a single notion: "What is the question?"

"To believe or not to believe, that is the question. You were born to it, Joseph. Just do your job," she said, releasing him.

He immediately took the napkin from Violet's Friendly Tavern out of his shirt pocket, unfolded it, and then turned his head away from her to wipe his mouth. He stared through the side window, but saw nothing but his own thoughts tripping through his mind as he ran the napkin from his lips, to his brow, and then back to his mouth. He felt everything but her presence, and there was no point in looking back because he knew that she would be gone. And true to his increasing knowledge of such things, she was.

Debbie Marshall stopped her car alongside Joe's cruiser. She had her family with her, two boys, two girls, and a husband who displayed his thoughts openly. Stretched over his right bicep in red, white, and blue ink was a vivid tattoo that read: DEATH BEFORE DISHONOR. Nobody doubted its meaning. He was not native to Toussaint, but you could never tell that by his words, which were few but as honestly spoken as his tattoo.

"You look like you've just seen a ghost," he said.

"No ghost, I've just been running on empty the past few days," Joe coughed out while still wiping his mouth with the napkin.

"Are you all right, Chief?" Debbie hollered over from the driver's seat, concerned over his unusual behavior.

"Affirmative," he said, rolling the napkin into an untidy ball and then discreetly tucking it beneath the floor mat.

"You better go home and get some rest," she said with a motherly tone. "You never know what the nighttime brings."

Joe looked past her husband's flexed bicep to the worried frown on her face. "You think so?"

Debbie's husband looked over to his wife and then looked back to Joe. "She's right, Blue. You look like hell."

Joe gave a modest shrug of his shoulders. "It must be the company I keep."

"Thanks a lot, Chief, you're a real peach," Debbie shot back as she delivered a short left jab to her husband's arm.

"Just kidding, Debbie, it's been a long shift," Joe grumbled, collecting his official self by sitting taller in his seat. "Don't worry, Dispatcher. I'll be ready for whatever the night brings."

"You better listen to her, Blue. She packs a wallop," her husband laughed, raising his eyebrows and widening his eyes so Joe alone could witness his mocking expression.

Debbie massaged her husband's arm with the offending hand. "I'll see you on patrol tonight."

"Affirmative," Joe answered as they drove away.

Debbie didn't leave her worry behind her. "The chief just doesn't look like himself. I hope he's okay?"

Her husband reached down and gave a firm squeeze followed by two pats to her right thigh. "It's been a tough weekend, darling. Joe's a good man. He just needs a little rest."

Debbie nodded as they passed the smoldering sign. "Without a doubt."

Joe looked at his reflection in the side mirror; he agreed with Debbie and her husband. He looked tired, and with his top shirt button unfastened and without a tie beneath his collar, he looked off the record even though this was his usual habit. He had the same regard for top buttons and ties as he did for clothes while sleeping; they never suited him. While his chest rose and fell beneath the stiff embrace of his authority, he unfastened the second button; now he was off the record. He reached down on his lap, picked up the stick, and then turned it between the fingers of both hands. After seven wheels of the stick, he placed it back on the seat beside him and then pulled away from the curb with the bitter taste of the day still in his mouth.

He continued west on Water Street until he reached the sign. One fire truck was still on the job with two firemen standing dutifully next to its perfectly groomed body. The early morning excitement had dwindled down to these two vigilant volunteers who were trained in all manners of firefighting. Joe stopped and hollered out his window.

"Keep your eyes open, gentlemen."

"No sweat, Chief," they both shouted back.

Joe managed a sincere but tired smile and then turned the corner for home. He respected men who stayed on the job, seeing it through, doing what they were trained to do. It was men like this, their women, and their children that made keeping the peace such a pleasure. Outside of Toussaint, he believed that men like this were rare, and women who understood them were rarer still, perhaps as rare as the two ethereal beings who moved about on a whim. Where did they come from? Where do they go to? Even though he had seen them, they were outside of any measure of his experience to explain; bourbon-drinking, beautiful, good-smelling beings from beyond were not his usual companions. If they were angels, they were certainly not what his people expected. If they were demons, they were certainly not what he expected. If they were other than those two imaginings, then he had no expectations at all. The moment only allowed a confirmation without explanation, and he was running with it. He had, the days of knowing, to cover the distance.

Joe arrived at the stone road that weaved through the tall grasses leading to his back door. The low-land flora was in bloom. He welcomed the vivid colors of swamp and meadow that were painted onto the land from May's palette. The transformation of the wetlands from winter's somber gray to spring's vibrancy was one of the awaited things. The time between the vernal equinox and the summer solstice was a probable condition that arrived on truth, not hope. It was the kind of change that Joe could live with. The budding of the fields and the flight of the rainbow-feathered birds that migrated through the marsh were expected and always arrived.

Unlike the strangers, May did not suddenly appear and challenge you to accept its variable personality, although they did have that in common. May was a bipolar expressionist, painting with mystic shifts of beauty with one pleasing hand and then destroying that beauty with its other cruel hand. The glorious sprouting of the land could easily fall prey to the killing winds of the Arctic shifts, or wither beneath the northern frost. All had to endure the artist's whim; the living had to adapt or die. The choice was simple. It was the kind of change that produced the hearty roots and resilient makeup of plant and beast. It was the kind of change that Joe could endure, the time of its arrival fitting somewhere within the limits of the lengthening day. No one could predict the exact hour of its appearance, but when it showed up, it could be embraced or met head-on, unlike the fickle omens of the two beings who most likely didn't fret over changes in the weather. Perhaps a change in the weather was just what Joe needed to thicken Toussaint's skin. He would not pray for a late snow, but he imagined that such a condition would be helpful. Eleven inches of frozen powder would be enough to keep Toussaint locked down for five days, holding the outsiders at bay. He would be thankful for such a reprieve. It would give him time to consider the breadth of all possibilities before lowering his shoulder against the rush. The days of knowing, had no order or number to count, but five days could be calculated; five days he could understand. He just had to find his pace.

The time that was created by man to name the hours was moving as kept time does, in predetermined cadence, calibrated by precise seconds within the timepieces designed to keep it. But the time beyond man was counting down in disordered, folded moments that lay one on top the other, hiding all but the last thing remembered. What was once common to all was quickly mutating into a harvest of the unusual, where men and women were challenged beyond reason to make sense of things that flowed in a nameless rhythm to an irregular beat. Just before twenty-three hundred hours, Debbie Marshall reported for work, shaking the snow from her hair.

"Whew," she whistled through her lips. "This weather will be the end of us."

"Do you think so, Mrs. Marshall?" the rookie dispatcher asked, angling for agreement with his own dark thoughts. "It's been insane around here since the chief fished that lady out of the water."

"Don't worry about it, son. We are on pathfinder duty. You know what I mean?"

"Yes, ma'am, I do, but..."

"There are no buts on pathfinder duty, only eyes and ears that use facts to find our way."

"I understand, Mrs. Marshall, but..."

"No buts, son. There are three kinds of words that move us in this world: the loving kind, the crying kind, and the fighting kind. We need the loving kind today. You know what I mean?"

"I do know what you mean, Mrs. Marshall, but we are having the craziest weather in history, and the chief and that woman are in the eye of the storm."

"That's why we need the loving kind of words right now. We are on pathfinder duty, the center of all communication for public safety. We have to keep the roads open. If you do what's right, maybe you can earn your wings tonight."

"Earn my wings? So you do believe in all this talk about angels and the wrath of God?"

"Just do your job, son. God and angels will take care of themselves, but they won't take care of the roads. That's our job. How many plows are in service? Are all of the roads passable? Are all of the emergency volunteers on standby? Do you have a linkup with the county? These are the real questions that pathfinders answer. We have to keep the village open, get the people to work, get the school buses moving in the morning, solve problems, and be productive. That's what we do in this office. If you can keep things moving, you will earn your wings like a good little angel. It's just an expression...just an expression..." She lingered over her words while hanging her down-filled parka on the oak hall tree that wobbled toward her on century-old legs.

"The chief hasn't logged in tonight," he said, giving Debbie one more opportunity to school him before removing her boots.

"What you mean is," she said, sitting down on the spindle-back chair that creaked and groaned with her slightest movement, "the chief never logged out this afternoon."

"That's right, he didn't," he said with a rookie's pained embarrassment. "He never called in, but how did you know that?"

"I know the chief," she answered while untying her boots. "If he didn't log in tonight, that means he's still on the job from this morning."

"You must know him pretty good, Mrs. Marshall."

"I do. We graduated from the same class in high school. I know him as a friend first and then as the chief. In both cases, he doesn't leave you hanging. If he didn't call in, then he's still on the clock. Blue Water can run for days without looking back. That's just the way he is, and nothing much will change him."

Debbie let out a big puff of air as she lifted her huge leather purse onto her lap. It was the size and shape of a burlap gunnysack with a rawhide tie that kept it closed. It was suitable for carrying most anything, and storing most everything, that a prepared mother of four needed when she left her home. She untied the purse, removed a green towel, and then placed it on the floor next to the chair. She removed her boots and then placed them side by side on the towel.

The young man watched closely, curious as to what other mysteries a lady's handbag might reveal. Debbie reached inside her bag, and just like Santa Claus, she pulled out a brand new pair of speedy-looking running shoes from its unfathomable bottom.

"I love these sneakers," she squealed girlishly before lacing up her size-five feet into the high-tech footgear. "They keep me in the race."

The rookie smiled as he cleaned his part of the day from the desk. He liked everything about his job, but he particularly liked working with Debbie Marshall. In his young mind, she was a trusted advisor, a great teacher, a stylish whirlwind of energy, and she was funny and cute, for a woman who had lived long enough to call cross-trainers "sneakers." When he finished clearing the desk, he poured the stale, burned coffee into the sink and then started a fresh pot brewing. He was eager to please this woman he thought so much about, even when he wasn't working. As she took her place behind the desk, he stood next to the coffeemaker, solemnly waiting for the last drop to fill the pot. His eyes were on the dripping brew, but his mind was somewhere between the excitement of the weekend and his desire to prepare a fitting cup of coffee that she would appreciate. When that moment finally arrived, he poured his hopeful expectations into a cup and then delivered it to her desk, along with a pan of gingerbread that was freshly delivered from home.

"Here you go, Mrs. Marshall. My mom brought it in just before the snow started falling. She made it just a few hours ago. I know it's your favorite," he said, politely placing the gingerbread and the coffee in front of her.

"What a nice surprise. How did you know that gingerbread is my favorite?"

"I pay attention, ma'am. Isn't that what pathfinders do?"

"You really are a sweetheart," she said, lowering her head over the pan and whiffing in the spicy aroma. "How about we share a piece before you log out?"

"No thanks, ma'am. My mom said to keep my fingers out of it. She has a late supper waiting at home, and I'm pretty sure that she made extra."

"Well you give your mom a big hug from me, and you tell her how much I appreciate her thoughtfulness."

"For sure," he said as he picked up the microphone. "To all officers in the field, Dispatcher Debbie Marshall will be taking command of the station. The time is twenty-three hundred." He spoke with an affected, deep resonance that would have been laughable had he not been so earnest.

"Well the apple doesn't fall far from the tree," she said, taking the microphone from his hand. "Dispatcher Marshall on duty, and I'll be taking calls all night. There's a hundred miles of bad road out there, so y'all take care. The time is still twenty-three hundred." Debbie and the rookie both raised their eyebrows at her casual report. So much was moving outside of everybody's control that even their usual behavior was an afterthought.

Debbie cut a large slice of the gingerbread. Eating out of her left hand while sipping coffee from her right, she savored the spicy taste. "This is wonderful," she mumbled with a mouthful of the stuff. "It's heavenly; there's nothing like it on this earth." She thanked the young man a few more times between bites and swallows before he left the station. The sound of the door closing was a dull thud as it settled against the snow that collected in the jamb. She thoroughly enjoyed the gingerbread, but she wished that she had some whipped cream to spread over the top. It was going to be a long night; whipped cream would have sweetened her taste for it.

After several hours of petitions and barefoot miles carved into the Persian rug, Nate removed his uniform, pulled a faded Volunteer T-shirt over his head, stepped into a twenty-year-old pair of tired jeans, and then headed over to Joe's. Although he didn't hear any voices, he thought that God was telling him to get moving.

Joe spent the length of his afternoon thinking about things that he understood and things that he could not comprehend yet was still willing to consider. He did not sleep, eat, or do anything to nourish his body for the coming hours. Looking outside his windows, he contemplated the afternoon sun and then the pearls of western light that dissolved into dusk upon the land. As the eastern shadows lengthened upon the fallen snow, the improbable was no longer unexpected. The natural rhythm of earthly things was interrupted by the bizarre and discordant sounds of a world disturbed. With the odd moment becoming the common extreme, order could not be kept and the peace could not be served. If there was something for Joe to do, he was still looking for it when Nate arrived at his door.

There are things that men talk about, and there are things that they dare not speak. There are things that men understand, and there are things that are accepted before they are given proof. For the remaining hours that Joe had before going back out on the road, Nate talked about all of these things, and Joe listened. He talked until the snow blanketed Toussaint with eleven inches of cover, which gave credence to his piety. When it was time for Joe to return to the road, he asked Nate to ride with him; Nate accepted. There was no doubt in Nate's mind what was coming. There was no question left unanswered, and he was glad to be a part of it. The feeling was not shared by Joe.

Chapter 8

The National Weather Service in Cleveland noted the anomalous conditions over Toussaint, but could not interpret the data with any reasonable explanation for its existence. In a hurried communication to the National Oceanic and Atmospheric Administration's main headquarters in Silver Spring, Maryland, the Cleveland office reported the following: "Toussaint, Ohio is encompassed within a deviant mass of twisting snowfall that is antithetical to current atmospheric conditions outside the village."

When asked to clarify the message, the Cleveland office replied: "It is an enormous vertical storm of unknown origin with cyclonic winds estimated beyond the nineteen thirty-four Mount Washington standard of two hundred thirty-one miles per hour. There is no supporting supercell activity associated with this event, and the International Satellite Communications System reports that the top of the storm extends beyond their ability to track. The surface winds are stationary, counterclockwise, saturated with heavy snow, and impervious to the radiant waves of our recording instruments. We cannot analyze it beyond a visual observation, and using what we know, it appears that the storm extends above the troposphere. Like our instruments, all radio and phone communication within the ground parameters of this occurrence is negative. This is a huge and historically unique event. We have no contact with Toussaint. We are helpless, and it is frightening. If the apocalypse is not upon us, it is surely upon Toussaint."

Word of Toussaint fell along the ground, tumbling and rolling into what could and could not be. Any vision of the outside world entering the village limits was blinded by the hand that delivered the snow. Toussaint was in climatic lockdown, taking care of its business, unaware that they were sitting exactly where Joe Water did not want to be, at the center of the world's attention, in the eye of the storm.

As Joe navigated his cruiser over terrain that was impassable to every soul but him, he breathed easier knowing that, somehow, his thoughts for more time were duly honored. He had a duty to perform, and whether by coincidence or supplication, he received the protracted moment and proceeded with due resolve. He drove with a sureness that represented all things that were known to be common to his nature while tapping a confident cadence with his fingers upon the wheel. He was unafraid, and with Nate riding shotgun, he was closing the distance on the unexplained. Nate, however, was silent in the cruiser. It was the kind of noisy silence that crackled when the wheels in a man's head were turning, the kind of raucous silence that spit and fumed when broken by any thought given to spurious examination. As they rolled closer to Twin Bridges, Nate spoke straight, in the way an honest man speaks when a friend is listening. It was the only talk sincere enough to calm the nagging quiet in his head.

"This freeze is going to kill the migration. We are witnessing an act of God, Blue. This is not nature acting on its own. This is God, commanding nature to abide by his will. Are you scared, or are you prepared, Blue?"

Joe hunched himself over the wheel. "Neither... Keep your eyes open for the turnoff. I want to take a look at the point."

"Why?"

"I'll know when I get there."

"There's nothing here for us, Blue. It's all snowed under."

"We'll see..." Joe left the west side of the road where he was certain the turnoff was located. He drove slowly through the groaning and popping snowpack until his cruiser could no longer crawl. He stopped and then reversed a few feet, rocking the vehicle back and forth to improve his line of retreat if he needed one. Confident in their ability to exit, he put the transmission in park, switched on the dome light, boosted the heater up a notch, cracked his window, and then opened the microphone to the dispatcher.

"This is your chief of police. I am still on the job."

"Affirmative, Chief, do you need a time stamp on your call in?" Debbie answered on the other end.

"Negative, I think that we all know what time it is?"

"Affirmative, Chief, God bless you."

"Maybe," Joe answered, and then he hung the microphone on the hook.

"What do you really know about God?" Joe said, turning his attention to Nate.

"I know that he has his hand in all of this."

"How can you be sure? Did he arrive on a cloud and let you in on his plan?" Joe said sincerely, without mocking his friend. "Did you see his face? Did you hear his voice? Perhaps he whispered it in your ear; would you know it if he did? Would you recognize his voice or confuse it with the wind and assume that he was speaking? Think for yourself, Nate. Know yourself, and if God is out there, he will know you too because you are too good to miss, buddy boy," Joe continued, earnestly seeking to glean the chaff of Nate's religion from the wheat of his faith.

"Forgive him, Father, for he knows not what he says," Nate said, shaking his head.

"I do know. I know that a lie gets a head start on the truth, but the truth always catches up. You cannot outrun the truth no matter how fast you are, not even you, buddy boy, with your record-setting moccasins tearing up the track."

"Well I think that it has caught up to us, and it's right in front of your eyes?"

"The only truth that I see is right here," Joe said, gripping the stick in his right hand.

"Jesus, Mary, Mother of God, what are you saying? Make sense, Blood."

"This stick is a piece of the oldest living thing on the planet. Imagine that, Nate, the oldest living thing. The very same tree that gave up this limb still lives, and it does so better than any other plant or animal in existence, including us. That's what I call the truth. That's what I call survival," Joe explained as he held up the stick for Nate's inspection.

"Oh brother, it's just a stick, Blue."

"It's more than a stick when you understand the heart of it. Your grandfather knew its teaching; I wanted to learn its lessons, you chose another path, and that's why he gave the stick to me."

Nate snatched the stick from Joe's hand, touching it for the first time since he was a boy; Joe did not resist. Nate studied the stick, holding it close enough to his face that he could smell the sticky pine aroma of its primordial past. He was curious, but not beyond belief. He turned it in his hand, examining the texture and look of the stick, and the way its shadow fell across the dashboard from the dome light's illumination. He considered what he thought to be every possibility for the stick's weighty appeal to Joe's sensibilities, but only found what he was looking for. He handed the stick back to Joe.

"It's just a stick, Blue. It's only a stick that was made by God."

"It is more than a stick, as you are more than the man that I see before me," Joe said, handling the stick in the reverential manner accustomed to him. "You are everything that has gone before you and continues within you, Nate, everything. Every action by blood or experience is who you are, and that is much more than what I see. Your ancestors believed that this was sacred ground, and you were born into that belief, and it is still a part of you, even though you have accepted another man's religion for your own. Your blood worshipped this land, raised their children here, fought to hold on to it, and died defending it. This land should be venerated; it is consecrated in their blood, the blood of the Shawnee, your blood. This is what I see when I consider this stick, all that has gone before me, not just what stands in front of me. You are Shawnee—Nathan Swift, blood of Tecumseh and the Great Prophet Tenskwatawa and the countless warriors before them. If God hears your voice, he should hear it in the language of your blood, the collective unconscious of your soul, giving consideration to all of you, not just the part of you that worships him. This is what makes sense to me. This is what I see when I hold this stick in my hand. This is the truth as I know it, and this is why it was given to me."

"That's pretty deep, Blue, deeper than the snow that's going to take us before God does, if you don't hustle up with your business here."

"You didn't hear me, did you?"

"That's not the voice I recognize, Blue. You are getting pretty wordy. Maybe God is speaking through you, but I still think that you should be praying."

"It's tough to change a mind that's set." Joe pulled a wool watch cap down over his ears, zipped up his down-filled field jacket, stuffed his big hands into his tight-fitting leather gloves, and then opened the door into the bitter cold. He stood up and looked around into the night. "You are Shawnee, Nate. Isn't that enough?" He turned and shined the flashlight into his friend's face.

Nate squinted into the glare of the light. "You better start praying, Blood."

"You better know what you're praying for. Sit tight," Joe said, closing the door with a dull thud.

Lowering his head against the rush of intense snowfall, there was no design to Joe's purpose, no reason beyond the idea that something might be out there, some confirmation that he was heading in the right direction, if there was a direction to take. This was the ground where it had all started, and if he walked it tonight, anything could happen. It was not his usual method of operation, but it was suitable to him now, considering that very little was routine, common, or predictable. Placing one foot in front of the other was a good way to go; there was always clarity in moving forward.

He strode through the flawless white powder until he reached the stooped cattails at the water's edge. He stopped and looked upon the rush of open water that swept around the point in urgent swirls of white-capped foam. If the weather held, it would take a few more days to freeze over the river enough to walk on. It would crackle and groan a little, but it could support a man's weight. Joe knew the changeable nature of water, the safe time and the unsafe time to test its support. He looked straight down into its liquid condition, and knowing the killing side of its swift current before a freeze, he still stepped off the point, one foot in front of the other, trying to find a good way to go.

Nate waited a few minutes in the cruiser, grabbed the extra flashlight from the glove box, and then followed his friend into the stabbing snow. Placing his own feet into each of Joe's footprints as though only one man had left them, he carefully walked inside Joe's straight and deliberate steps. It was a perfect trail to follow until they ended on the water's edge. Nate swept the area with his light and found nothing. There were no return tracks or any lateral signs of movement along the shoreline. There was nothing but the falling snow, the river, and the sound of it all colliding with the marshland on the point; there was no sign of Joe. Nate believed that which was true; there was no place for Joe to be but back in the heart-stopping bitterness of the river.

He sprinted eastward along the banks where the tidal waters left the remains of storm-broken life, screaming Joe's name, searching the water with his small beam of light. He burst over the spill of rocks and wooden debris dumped in tangled heaps, now an unseen hazard under the cover of snow; he had no heart for prudence. Trampling through the perilous leftovers of displaced and ruined things, Nate raced recklessly along the marshland, shouting and praying for what he was sure God could deliver, but might be holding out on him. Within a few moments, he made his way to where the backwaters chopped furiously beneath Twin Bridges; nothing could stop his advance. If God wouldn't answer him now, he was going to take matters into his own hands. Quickly shedding his boots and coat, he flexed his knees to dive over the boulders and fallen limbs that were between him and the river.

"Forgive me, Lord, but if you're still with me, then help me!" he shouted, and then a strong hand grabbed his shoulder and spun him around.

"I told you to sit tight," Joe said firmly, without shouting.

"Blue, where were you?" Nate screamed loud enough to shake off some of the snow that was frozen to his brow.

"I have always been here."

Nate was breathing heavily; his face, a painted-freeze of winter white. "Jesus...Joe..."

Joe picked up Nate's stiffened boots from the ground and handed them to his friend. "Grab your gear, and let's get moving. We have work to do."

"Jesus...Joe...what happened?" Nate wiggled his frosted toes back into his boots.

"The river's not frozen."

"Is that a revelation?" Nate shook off the cold as he zipped up his coat.

"It was a revelation to me," Joe answered as the two of them headed through the snow-packed brush back to the cruiser, with Nate following closer this time in Joe's tracks. Step by identical step, Joe led and Nate followed toward the welcoming sound of the cruiser's steady idle beneath the heavy cover of snow.

"She's alive and running, and my feet are freezing," Nate said, lifting his feet outside of Joe's tracks and then marching through the drifts around the front of the vehicle while Joe quietly cleared the snow from his window with his gloved hand.

"Are you afraid that we won't measure up?" Nate asked, removing the snow on his side in the same manner.

"What is there to fear in a life except that it is not well lived? We protect and serve; what could be better than that? Buckle up," Joe said as they opened their doors to the welcome warmth of the idling cruiser.

Debbie Marshall leaned away from the microphone. She took another bite of gingerbread and chewed slowly as the snow continued to bury Toussaint beneath an errant prayer. In her years at the desk, the chief had never refused an official time for his coming or going. Knowing this, and understanding more about Joe Water than most, she picked up a pen and then marked the official time into the record. It seemed like the right thing to do.

Joe backed the cruiser over the faint remains of its rutted trail until he reached the trackless road ahead. The snow was dropping out of the sky in plump bodies the size of soap bubbles from a child's plastic wand, reducing the visibility to the lighted space that glowed blue along the front edge of his hood. Clutching the wheel, Joe concentrated on the condition of Twin Bridges as they passed over its treacherous surface, holding tight to who he had always been. Safely crossing the river, he continued down the road in a slow but deliberate approach to the village, looking for everything but seeing nothing beyond what was right in front of him. With only an arm's length of lighted distance ahead, a songbird fell hard against the windshield. Its red and yellow feathers, matted and stiff, made the noise of a pitched ball into a catcher's mitt as it impacted the glass. Then another ball of feathers fell upon the hood, a frozen blue body that bounced twice as it ricocheted over the roof. Without pause, and colliding from every angle, a flurry of rebounding colors smashed against the cruiser with death-dealing force. A feathered cacophony of green, orange, black, and gray corpses reported their deaths with the loud snapping of bones and fractured claws scraping over the paint. Their frozen forms sizzled and cracked like colored cubes popped out from some ice tray in the sky.

"Jesus!" Nate said through clenched teeth while rubbing his crucifix between the thumb and forefinger of his right hand. "What's happening?"

Joe did not answer as the birds continued falling in a sickening cadence that thumped along in a funeral dirge. Warblers, vireos, hummingbirds, shorebirds, and birds of prey, fated to the impulse of favors received, were picked before their time from the night sky and sent bouncing and rolling, spiked into a littered mess of torn feathers and dead flesh.

"Jesus!" Nate repeated, applying more pressure to his crucifix. "This snow is killing the migration for sure."

As each bird met its mortal limit, Joe realized one thing about a God who answers prayer: you better be careful what you pray for. The distance between Joe's home and the village was just a few miles, but on this night, it could only be measured in such thoughts.

"You can't deny the meaning of this, Blue."

"No, I can't."

Nate tucked his crucifix down the collar of his shirt. "That's it? That's all that you have to say?"

"The biggest week in American birding is going to be a bust this year."

"Jeez, Joe, that isn't funny."

Joe looked over at his friend and smiled. "I'm glad I'm not a bird." The drive that could be measured in such thoughts was getting shorter.

Outside of Toussaint, the actions of mankind were stirred within the pot of their desires. Some were noble in their efforts to serve others; some were quick to serve themselves. As the migratory birds of Toussaint were falling to their cold and helpless deaths, six computer-guided aircraft from the Office of Naval Research entered the airspace surrounding the village, froze, and then disappeared into the coiling winds, unable to adapt, unprepared to survive. The National Weather Service then opened the Emergency Broadcast System and ordered every citizen in Ottawa County to seek immediate shelter. Within moments of the broadcast, the forces were mobilized and dispatched to secure every road leading into Toussaint. Blocking every point of entry, the emergency crews were given the command and the authority to keep everybody off of the roads. As word of the events spread, aroused by the rumors of flaming signs and prophetic winds, the national news media descended upon Ottawa County in a convoy of tech trucks and zealous journalists that fumed and flared behind the blockade. Unable to reach the scene of the storm, the reporters were screaming for First Amendment privileges as they stooped behind the barricades, drawing pitiful conclusions from rumored conditions in an effort to be first with breaking news reports. Releasing their loose notions via satellite to all points on the globe, they held the world's attention with each frustrated broadcast. The world was now watching Toussaint. It was a witch's brew of dread.

Joe and Nate turned onto Water Street, stopped the cruiser in the middle of the block, turned off the ignition, and then activated the reserve battery system. He switched on his red, white, and blue strobes, which could burn for at least seventy-two hours on reserve, leaving it the only man-made light left burning in town. The two men stepped into the street and then walked side by side to the station. When they arrived, Debbie Marshall was wrapped up in a red blanket, sitting in the sparkling glow of a lighted candle. She was eating gingerbread, drinking coffee, and waiting patiently for the power to return.

"I'm so glad to see you boys! That's one heck of a snowfall, Chief. There's no power in the village, and all backup systems are dead. My watch has stopped, my flashlight doesn't work, it's cold in here, and I can't get the furnace to operate. I can't even raise a holler on the radio. What's a girl to do?"

"Pray," Nate said while touching the crucifix beneath his shirt.

"You don't want to do that," Joe said. "Your prayers may be answered."

Chapter 9

By the time Coyote downed his last longneck, the snow had already covered his yard in a blowing sea of white drifts. He was reclining on the tired backseat that he had salvaged from his granddad's old Packard. The odor and feel of its woolen fabric was a reliable sentiment, the kind of treasured item that a man appreciates beyond a woman's sensibility to comprehend. The generously stuffed, musty-smelling antique was his center for savoring his past and reflecting on all things found at the bottom of a bottle. He was sitting in the dark with his feet propped up on a workbench, rolling the empty bottle back and forth over his uncovered white leg. It felt good to knead the angular muscle beneath his resurrected flesh. Working the bottle between the frayed edges of the blown-off pant leg and his skinny ankle at the top of his exploded boot, he imagined the crystalline white flakes tumbling in the air to be miniature angels from heaven.

It was not unusual for Coyote to dwell on the physical details of life. A sharp eye and creative hand were the hallmarks of his trade. He could listen to an idling engine and formulate a laundry list in his mind about the particulars of the vehicle's ignition timing, fuel-to-air ratios, and performance settings. Other mechanics deferred to him when they could not solve their own motorized mysteries. They called him "The Dynamometer Dog" because he never used an engine analyzer to sniff out the properties of a mechanical solution. Such a mind could do well when applied to all problems, seen or unseen in a life, but Coyote loved cars and trucks. Until today, he had no reason to expand the range of his thinking. Until today, snow was just a cold, wet deliverer of stalled cars for his business. Now, the snow was much more to consider.

As deep as a man can dig beneath the surface of his existence, Coyote worked the ground of his mortal life. He leaned forward, leaving an impression of his thoughtful self in the squashed material of the seat. He placed the longneck on top of the workbench, pulled open the bottom drawer, and then removed a wax-sealed bottle of bourbon. It was a gift from a satisfied customer, stashed untouched with some other collectibles since last Christmas. He wasn't much of a whiskey drinker, and the bottle felt unfamiliar in his hand, so he broke the seal, twisted the cork from the bottle, and then poured the distilled solution into his empty beer bottle until it rose to the top of the neck like mercury in a thermometer. Now he had something in his hand that had a more familiar feel. It was good bourbon for a good man, but when he took his first tug from the bottle, he shook his head and made a sound from his lips like a man drowning in a tub and then sat down with a thud, forcing seventy-year-old dust from the seat's past. The quality spirit was a bad influence on the good man. With the snow piling up over the windows, and the temperature in the gridiron falling dangerously toward freezing, Coyote exhaled short, curling puffs of air, trying to form rings of frozen vapor through his pursed lips. Instead, the exhaled air looked more like car exhaust from an engine that was missing on a few cylinders. Failing to create the desired effect, he took another swallow and then followed it with a deep and low-pitched growl, revving up the old Coyote in the pit of his gut, where the liquor mixed poorly with his thoughts.

After too many swallows in the dark, followed by the mournful blend of animal wailing and a man's lament, Coyote was convinced that the snow marked the sure beginning of the end for everybody. Throwing the back of his wobbly head into the cushy stuffing of the old car seat, he let out a howl that only a lonely dog would cry. It was important to be sociable, to be running with the pack, when such a snow was collecting around a man's life. Those who ran with you should now curl around your weakness, sustaining you with the heat of their own lives, but Coyote was alone. Before his eyes closed to what remained of his world, he issued an inconsolable yelp and then slid slowly over to his left side, snoring loudly before his head landed in the seat.

"Tom, before you put a wrench on anything, you listen to what the motor is telling you. Follow your ears with your eyes, and they will tell your hands what to do. Do you understand, son?" The voice woke him up from a place in his spinning dreams.

Dad...Dad, he thought, but he could not answer as the gridiron revolved around him.

"Tommy-boy, you're a dagnab animal out there! You're like those junkyard dogs behind your old man's fence, but you're skinnier and wilder! You're a demented, deranged, maniacal canine, a lean, mean, bone-eating coyote. That's you, a coyote! Now you run across the middle, and Nate will hit you on the numbers. Catch the ball, Coyote, and then keep running with it. Score some points for us, son!"

No sweat, Coach, he wanted to answer, but he could not speak the words as he dug desperately into the seat for a handhold.

"Tommy, fix this radio for me, sugar. It's the gospel hour, and I'm getting nothing but static. Please, Tommy, you're the only one who can do it. I don't know what I'd do without you, baby boy."

Mom...Mom, he tried to answer, but the gridiron accelerated with dizzying velocity. As the full mixture of alcohol swirled through his brain, he was left with little choice but to hold on.

"Thomas, take my hand, and I'll lead you out of here. Trust me; take my hand," an unknown voice implored above all other thoughts in his head.

Inhaling the spirituous mixture of his own breath and the sweet aroma that now enveloped him, Coyote released his grip on the seat and stretched his arms toward the voice.

"That's a good boy, Thomas James. It's time for us to go," the voice said as Coyote felt two powerful hands grab him around the wrists and then lift him into the air. As his feet touched the floor, he opened his eyes as wide as he could to get a good look at the one who called him by his Christian name. She was made from every woman of his dreams and smelled like every pleasure he had ever tasted. Drunk or sober, he was a man who understood details, and hers were a fervid vision that few men could refuse. Without further examination, he balanced himself on uncertain footing. His thinking, displaced by a volume of liquor that he was not tempered to agree with, was muddled and confused. He was wobbly and unsure, but lost in the pleasure of her company. She was, without question, the nonpareil of female flesh. Her touch was amazingly strong yet exciting, all woman and inviting. Woozy and weak, ensnared in his own leghold trap of overindulgence, he steadied himself and tried to stand without her help; she would not release him.

"I can do this myself," he said as he shook his head from side to side.

"I am sorry, Thomas, but I have you now."

In spite of her fine lines and the tempting hold of her grip, he tried once more to release himself from her grasp; her resistance was sobering.

"You're that woman, aren't you?" he said, drinking her in with clearer vision.

She tightened her hold on him. "Yes, I am."

"Let loose of me now."

"I am sorry, Thomas, but you reached out for me. You are mine." She skimmed across the floor with Coyote digging his heels into the concrete. He was no match for the speed at which she moved or the strength of her embrace. Now that she owned him, he wanted to resist, but it did not matter. She passed through the open door with the blizzard whirling around them in white, freezing swells. She pulled him through the yard without effort, without losing the sweet, seductive aroma that clung to her like a morning mist. She lost neither her beauty nor her poise in her single-minded spectacle of dominion over him. She was in every way more beautiful and more appealing as she dragged him across the yard like a wind sock in a gale. Her prodigious strength and calm manner intensified Coyote's smitten feelings toward her, but he still tried to pull away.

He called to his dogs, but they did not answer, so he did what he always did when his excitement was too great to contain. "Yeeeooowww..." he howled as his feet left the ground. "Yeeeooowww...Let me go, lady, before I forget my manners." His voice was loud and clear, carrying over the night air, but she did not listen. She was in every way too much for the old dog to handle as they lifted off into the darkness.

The mystery of her no longer bewitched him. She was something to fear as he dangled between where he had been and where he was going. He was afraid and desperate to be set free, so he started praying, when prayer comes easiest to any man.

"Oh God, please give me the strength," he barely whispered as he sped through the air, twirling behind the dizzying fragrance of a woman he could not command. He felt helpless, and weightless, and terrified of his destination. He saw snowflakes turn into starlight, and starlight burst into a spreading white light that stretched into the dark space that he was being hauled into. The speed of his thoughts accelerated exponentially to include every detail of his living in instant repose, in silver-framed images. He felt the beginning and the end of his life being compressed into these moments. It was unfathomable and frightening beyond reason. If this was to be his death, he wasn't ready, he wasn't willing, and it just didn't feel right.

"Oh God, save me!" he cried out, and then he felt himself falling, tumbling breathlessly in his chilling descent. He was free, and he was no longer afraid, and his first thought was that if he could fall like this for the rest of eternity, it really wouldn't be such a bad thing. His last thought was that he really had to stop drinking, and then he hit the deepest part of the snow face-first, the way a drunken man always drops when he's had enough of standing.

Coyote was planted no more than seven feet from the gridiron's open door. His body was pushed deep into the cold white drift, arms and legs outstretched like the imprint of a snow angel made by a child. Facedown, unaware of his surroundings, unable to lift himself out of the wintry freeze, he did not stir. Except for his shallow breathing, he was motionless as the snow covered him beneath a soft crystal blanket; a flattened monument to why beer drinkers should never order from the top shelf.

When the dogs dug him out from under the snow, he was half frozen. Stiff and barely breathing, with shortened puffs of snotty vapor escaping his nose, he groaned when the stranger's strong arms lifted him up and carried him into his house. It was life that he had prayed for, and it was life that was delivered. Written on a note of despair, payable on demand to the holder, Coyote was now mortgaged up to the hilt.

Joe paced the station's floor, meditating in the way of water—empty mind, shapeless and formless, able to flow, able to crash, pouring him into whatever vessel was needed to protect his people. He was going to void himself of the unintended prayer, the weak-minded petitions that were offered up because he couldn't solve his own problems. Such prayers came with a devastating consequence when answered, and somebody out there, somewhere beyond his understanding, was listening and answering. His old knowledge served him well before the unknown juggernaut dialed in on Toussaint. He once had the solution to most of Toussaint's troubles. Either by thought or deed, he could reach a final outcome that was just, and fair, and final. To move in this way now was too perilous to consider; the logical conclusion skewed heavily toward chaos. He was suffering from his own humanity, unable to fathom the depths where these visitants bided, watching, aiding and abetting humanity. He wanted to be sure of his actions and not be left in the dark, where men of little faith reside, uneasy with the idea that there are things bigger than themselves. What he was beholding was bigger, greater than him in ways that an ordinary man cannot understand. That much he knew, so he paced the station's floor like water—empty mind, shapeless and formless, wanting to flow into whatever form he needed.

Coyote awoke faceup beneath the bleach-infused sheets of his bed. He remained still, staring toward the white ceiling, collecting his memories from the preceding day. Expecting the head-banging of a morning hangover, he was surprised by his overall good condition. Except for the colorful pulse of light that radiated throughout the room, it might just be another ordinary day. Watching as particles of dust danced through the rainbow of unfamiliar light, he was certain that this was not going to be a day of common things. The light deserved consideration, and he applied himself to it while studying the brushstrokes in the painted plaster. He did not move his head or twitch a limb as he passed his eyes over the surface of the ceiling and his textured beliefs. By lying still, he thought that the light might miss him, might not shine upon him, and maybe not notice him at all. It was too late to hide his head beneath the covers; he was already exposed. The smartest thing to do was to be motionless, to breathe silently, and to open his eyes and ears to what might be looking at him. After a long and labored study of everything above him, he let his eyes fall down to the source of the light at the foot of his bed, and then he closed them and pretended to sleep. Even a smart old dog like Coyote could be reduced to such a childish strategy in the light of revelation, and revelation was standing in the room. Like any man who accepts things that he cannot see, Coyote was uneasy about witnessing them in the flesh. Cleared of the whiskey fog, he was less sure how to deal with it.

"Thomas James," the voice from the light called, "open your eyes."

Coyote remained still. There was power in stillness, in the quiet of thought before action, in the meditative brainwork of knowledge. But no such thoughts were common to him today; he was just a scared dog afraid to greet his master. Too scared to move, too scared to discover what he always longed for. He was terrified, as even good men will be when they believe that they are facing their Maker. He kept his eyes closed, hoping to be overlooked on this day, wishing that his head was beneath the covers.

"Thomas, open your eyes and look at me."

"God help me!" Coyote shouted, squeezing his eyelids tighter.

"Do you think that someone should do for you what you can do for yourself, what you can see for yourself?"

"Who are you?" Coyote asked, squeezing his eyelids so tight that his wiry gray eyebrows touched the top of his cheekbones.

"Open your eyes, and you will see," the deep but gentle voice said, but Coyote would not look. He did not want to give in to this voice as he had given in to the voice of the woman. He did not want to experience the outcome of his beliefs, not now, alone in his bed. Keeping his eyes closed seemed to be the best choice; he just didn't want to see what was coming. But it never came.

"You are easily deceived. It is a weakness that all men share," the voice said with a sigh. "Your vanity and desire are easier to win over than your fear. Men are quick to move toward sugar. Much like flies, they consume the sweetness of it and then lay their seed all over what's left. If you want to trap a man, give him a taste of what is sweet. She was sweet, wasn't she?"

The voice remained gentle, but still not persuasive. Fear is a powerful force, more powerful than reason. It makes good men do bad things and bad men do worse. It is the body of the beast, and Coyote was beneath its claws.

"A frightened man is a destructive man," the voice said sadly. "He is a man filled with hate and anger. He is a man who doubts himself and all others, a useless man. What kind of man are you that you cannot even open your eyes?"

"Who are you?" Coyote asked again.

"I am who I am," the voice said so convincingly that Coyote lifted his head from the pillow.

It was a slight movement, a motion that was seasoned in the woods and brush fields of Ottawa County. It was the confident movement that put his hunter's instinct on full alert, prepared for something big, and then he opened his eyes and found it. The voice belonged to the same stranger who had appeared in the village, fiercely magnificent, darkly handsome, and with a kind expression that welcomed Coyote's trust. The light in the room radiated from his being, and the fragrance of his body was distinctively pleasant. He was so beautiful and smelled so good that Coyote was embarrassed to have noticed. Given his experience with the woman, he was hoping that he was at last looking at an honest-to-God angel, if not God himself. He just had to ask.

"Are you God?"

"I told you, Thomas, I am who I am. Get up! I have something for you to do." He handed him an unfamiliar cell phone. Small, and cut like a diamond with many facets, the phone seemed more suitable as a jewel on a necklace for a Catawba Island housewife than it did a communication device. It was funny-looking to Coyote, but he did not laugh.

"It is a simple thing, but it must be done properly, and it must be done by you. Just talk into the unit. You must make one call to someone who has the influence to assemble a gathering of your people. Make the right call, as this is the only one that you will be granted. Tell that person that we will all meet in the high school gymnasium, God is coming, don't be late. Do it only as it should be done."

Coyote obeyed because he believed that it was the right thing to do. Every instinct agreed; every good thought confirmed. He held the phone up in front of his face and asked for the police station. He knew that Debbie Marshall would answer and that she would fulfill the stranger's command. It was the right call to make.

Debbie was startled by the ringing. With all power out in the village, the phone was the last thing expected to be heard from. Joe and Nate were just as surprised as they watched her pick up the receiver.

"Toussaint Police Station, Dispatcher Marshall speaking."

"Hey, Debbie, I have a message for you."

"Coyote, is that you?"

"Yes, sweetheart, it's me. I don't understand much of this, so don't ask. All I know is that I have to give the word to you, and then you have to take it to everyone in the village. That's the deal, sweetheart. Everybody has to hear the word, and you're the only gal who can deliver it, so listen carefully to the word. The word is…God is coming, and he will meet us up at the high school, so don't be late. That's it. That's all of it. That's the word…" He said nothing more as his voice disappeared back into the infinite space from which it came.

"Coyote, can you hear me? Coyote…Coyote…" she yelled, but there was no answer.

The president of the United States grounded all incoming and outgoing international flights. He closed the seaports to all foreign vessels and then deployed the military to secure the land borders. It was an action that was expected, if not totally understood, by most of America's citizens. The nation could not endure the crush of foreign pilgrims on a religious journey toward Toussaint. America, the land that welcomed the poor, and the tired, and the huddled masses, had no room at the inn.

Chapter 10

Violet Love burst through the door of the station, glowing beneath the sparkle of snow that crowned her head. Her gusty arrival drew the blustery air over the candle flame, causing it to flicker and flash, lighting her face in a way that reminded Joe of the vaporous woman who had opened this Pandora's box of confusion. In the shimmering blush of the glimmering light, Violet looked beautiful, vital, and tempting; Joe looked away. He had no time for such thoughts, not today, maybe never.

"I saw your lights, Chief," Violet said, waving her arms across her body to brush off the snow and the exhilarating chill. "Everything man has put his hand to has stopped! There's no heat, no electricity, no way to call out of the village, every clock has stopped, but your lights are still flashing. I'm thinking it's another sign, don't you? Just like the burning words, the nor'easter, and now this snow. I'm not the first to recognize it, and I'd bet double up that your buddy Nate has clued you in a few times by now because he wouldn't keep his pocket change from you. There's no risk on the bet, and I don't even have to throw that woman or that gorgeous man on the table to cover my odds. It all points to you, Chief Joseph Water. All signs lead to you. You are the light and the way! It's just too funny, Joey. I saw your lights, and now I've found my way to you. God has a great sense of humor, don't you think? I'm not too crazy about his timing because I still had things to do like marriage, and children, and maybe you, Joey, maybe you? Bad timing, Joey, but I love his sense of drama. The buildup is fascinating…"

Joe kept his back to her as she spoke, so Violet circled around the desk to get his attention. The waving of her arms as she wheeled around the candlelight spun a shadowed image on the walls and ceiling that reminded Joe of a tottering winged angel closing in on him. He turned his head toward Debbie, who held the telephone tightly to her ear while spreading Coyote's news, and then he looked to Nate for support. They both appeared to be frozen in time, suspended in a space that he and Violet were not a part of. He had to say something, so he just dismissed her words, imagining her to be drunk, even though every word spoken was purposeful and clear.

"Keep your thoughts to yourself; you have had too much to drink. Talk to Debbie. You just saved her a call." Joe pulled his tight-fitting leather gloves over his knuckles. "I'm on the clock, and nothing's getting done with me standing around here. Nate, you stay with the girls, and pour some coffee into Violet, even if it's cold and bitter. Dry her out a little." He looked directly at his friend with his brown eye.

"I just can't believe you, Joe Water," Violet said, smiling and shaking her head.

"You should," Joe answered, winking his blue eye at her, and then he walked out into the tempest, leaving those he could trust to spread the news. Pulling his collar over his neck, he headed for the high school to make a place for their exodus to the gym.

The snow was spread generously over Toussaint's claim on the earth, a thick blanket of inexplicable glacial freeze that fell profoundly from a harvest heaven. There was no trace of man's tracks left on the ground, no road, sidewalk, or trail to be seen. Joe would be the first to lay his mark upon the land, a man to follow. In the near distance, he could hear the howling winds that kept the outside world in its place, away from Toussaint, giving him one tick more from the moment to find his way. Step by labored step, he lifted one leg and then the other, poking holes through heaven's white offering, knowing that the hours were being squeezed from his reprieve. He tried to pick up the pace of his stride, but the long slog through the deep snow was grievously slow. Seconds ran into minutes; minutes were hurrying the hour. His seasoned limbs, bearing the burden of four days without a restful sleep, complained with a well-known burn that told him he was working. At first he liked the noisy company, but the constant reminders were a redundant pain. With a mile behind him, he stopped for a moment to catch his breath, a rare condition for Joe when he was still carrying the ball. Bending over, he placed his hands on his knees and took long, deep breaths to satisfy his winded legs. Rubbing the sting out of his thighs, he was losing the joy of the burn. With the time left to him fading, each searing muscle growl smoldered into a weakened tissue groan. That's when he let the words slip away.

"Hey God, are these, the days of knowing? You can't be serious." Then he put his head down and pushed against the wind. With a mile to go and no time to spare, he heard a whooshing sound above the wind. It was the rustling of their wings.

From an amber cloud appeared two winged dazzlers that blazed golden against the eastern horizon of the night sky. Their sweet fragrance kissed his senses as they sailed over him, parting the snow with the muted beating of their wings, a smooth sound like the hushed folding of velvet into a drawer. Such visions would bring most men to their knees, submitting to the sublime, shivering in the cold, and then quaking with the unfathomable realization that such things could be real; but not Joe Water. Joe stood straight up and witnessed the undeniable wild wonders as their swift and powerful flight cleaved a path before him. Their work was clean and precise. No county crew could ever duplicate the supremely carved boulevard across the landscape, cut directly to the gymnasium's front door. Moving with unthinkable speed, they finished their calling and then flew back into the amber cloud, disappearing from all but Joe's memory.

"Thank you," he said. It was the first time that he thanked anyone he wasn't sure of. The evidence was building; the truth would be known soon enough.

It was now easier going for Joe, the trail ahead swept clear. Beneath his feet were the granite markers that paid homage to the bloodline of Toussaint. Engraved upon the polished pavers were the names of every known Volunteer who had lived and died and was buried beneath the village grass in grave sites along the Portage River. While they waited for the Day of Resurrection to reunite their souls with their living bodies, their memories were still full of life on the walkway to the school. Each paver was expertly cut and measured to be two hands in length by two hands in width. They were embedded in the ground in rows of twelve across and stretched the last half mile to the school. Joe was familiar with every name on every stone, starting with the newest of the departed that stretched immediately before him and ending with the names of the elders that were positioned respectfully in front of the school. Every life meant something; every soul counted.

Joe revered every name that was underfoot, so he stepped lightly over them. Such care might slow him down some, but the path was wide and clear, and his caution a necessary fact. He would never disrespect a memory in order to save time, not today, not the way he was feeling. He marched along on his toes, apologizing with every step until he reached the school's gymnasium. If God was going to call a meeting of his faithful, this would be the place. This is where their names led; this is where their hearts were. It did not surprise him to find that the doors were unlocked, the lights were on, and it was warm inside. Such remarkable things were becoming so ordinary that it seemed fitting. If the God that they believed in was coming, he wanted a warm house and a comfortable congregation, and he wanted Joe to be there first. Such things were no longer strange, and to a bone-tired Joe Water, they were not even worth considering. With the whole place to himself, he walked up to his reserved seat in the bleachers—row thirteen, seat thirteen—and then sat down and waited for the game to begin. He closed his eyes and once more meditated in the way of water—empty mind, shapeless and formless, flowing into sleep—but it was beyond the meditative mind where he slumbered.

Joe slept as a man sleeps when he is weary and troubled by life. With his back against the hard wooden bench behind him, he slipped away to where fears are kept. In the lonely, darkest pool of slumber's fitful domain, in the place where images of heaven and hell pour lucid dreams that could drown a man as he sleeps, Joe fell into the depths. Submerged in the crazy distortions of real and unreal things, suffocating in the murky waters of dread, he tried to wake himself, to shout himself into sensible awareness, but the groan that he issued was not even strong enough to lift his head…to open an eye…to relieve him from the terrible heaviness that was sitting on his chest...squeezing his body as he struggled to move.

"Be still, Joseph. I am here for you," she said with a merciful tincture of feeling, but the suggestive and sweet aroma that flavored her with unspoken pleasure said different. "Joseph, Joseph, Joseph." She sighed with reassuring comfort, but the warm and humid fervor of her body betrayed her. Her breath was upon him, steamy and alive, speaking into his right ear. "Joseph, oh Joseph, you have been waiting for me your whole unbroken life. I am the one you longed for when you could not awaken from sleep, when you dreamed of removing your human skin and you found it calming to be naked. Do not deny, it Joseph; I was there with all of your secrets. It was always me and no one else." Weakened by every impulse that betrays a man's good intentions, Joe struggled to renounce her as she wrapped herself around his thoughts and his body.

The air was pregnant with the deluding spice that seasoned every word with the knowledge of him. Joe turned his head away from her assurances, but she was all around him, and even if he could find the strength within him to leave, he had no place to go. He was at the mercy of this divine dream that was sitting on his chest, and though he knew her to be false, he could not cast her off. In the deepest, darkest, fitful pit of his sleep, his strength would have to come from some other place, from someone else.

"Wake up and be a man, Joseph. Know me, and I will be yours forever." She pressed herself hard against him and then circled the tip of her pink tongue around his open mouth, causing him to gag from the wet intrusion. "Forever," she sighed as she probed with serpentine persuasion, tasting the salt that was rising from his skin, possessing control of him, bringing forth the teasing hunger before it is satisfied. "Forever," she squealed victoriously, smacking her wet lips together, savoring the human scent that issued from his pores. Then she began rocking with the furious delight that she was about to receive what she came for. But Joe wasn't giving…

"You're no angel!" Coyote shouted from behind her as he locked his arms around her neck and tried pulling her backward. "Remember me? Get off of him, you black-hearted wench!" He twisted her head like he was throwing a bull. "You don't belong here, and we don't want you." He pulled hard enough to wrestle her attention away from Joe. She started to vibrate, but Coyote held fast, and when she spun around to toss him, he jumped on her naked back and dug his knees into her ribs.

"Get off of me, little man!" she hissed through clenched teeth.

"Y'all don't have what it takes, sister. I'm gonna ride ya to the moon." Winding her hair around his left hand, Coyote then slapped her on the bottom with the palm of his right hand. "Let's ride, Jezebel!"

Wings sprouted from her back as she rose into the air with Coyote's arms and legs wrapped around her like ribbon on a Christmas gift. The release of her impassioned weight was liberating, rousing Joe to the sight of them wrestling in the air. The whole of her body was perceived, bare and struggling, sending forth a deafening buzz that accelerated beyond noise into a realm of anguished voices that screeched and bawled. Joe rose to his feet while covering his ears as Coyote held doggedly to the beautiful, shrieking siren. Coupled together, she bucked and spun and crashed Coyote against the ceiling. She beat her wings against his head and then dropped toward the floor in a death spiral before soaring back up into the rafters, but Coyote's persistence was equal to her resistance. He was holding on for Toussaint, and he was digging in and riding hard.

As Joe witnessed the ravishing creature spinning wildly in the air, trying to dislocate his friend's body parts, he recognized her, but not by name. She came by so many denominations that he almost called her "Money," but that was not a fitting name for one who was so disturbingly desolate. You could get change from money, but this woman would never change. She was wonderfully tempting, but maniacally self-indulgent, angel food cake wrapped around a devil's food center.

"Avaricious!" he shouted. "Come down here with my friend!"

She laughed when he called to her, mocking his demand, but then she tumbled from above with her wings beating hysterically against the air that would not support her. What command and beauty she had was lost in the revelation of her design. Joe knew her, and she was not getting her way. She hit the floor hard with Coyote still gripping her body.

"Jesus, that was some ride. Should I let loose of her now?"

"You really are a rube, Thomas," she said, struggling to her knees, and then she let out a wail, a sonic scream, but Coyote held fast.

"Release her," Joe said.

"Whatever you say, Blue." But before he did, Coyote gave her one more squeeze for the road.

"You skinned my knees, you hick," she complained as she stood up and then bent over to rub her reddened skin. There was something pitiful about her now, something so sad that Joe was moved to be merciful.

Coyote just stared at the sumptuous rise and fall of her flesh, remembering how she felt in his hands, not forgetting the consequences of her touch.

"Hold your hands up, palms facing me," Joe demanded.

Resigned to Joe's command, she immediately obeyed, holding both palms up for inspection. Joe looked her over with both eyes fixed on the skin of her open hands. She had prints on the willowy tips of her fingers, and fine lines marking the folds of her lithe joints and playing in varying patterns across her palms. She was different than the stranger. It was one more thing for him to consider.

Coyote had his fill of consideration. "There's no momma's milk in this mare; there's only poison."

"Beautiful," Joe said.

"Beautifully toxic, Blue. Don't be forgettin' that."

"Indeed," Joe murmured as he removed his coat and wrapped it around her body.

"You soiled my wings, you bumpkin." She continued her grievance against Coyote as Joe's coat covered her facts. "You will never achieve immortality in culture in this petri dish you call a home. You will be swallowed up by the hungry that are eager to gnaw on your bones."

Coyote threw his hands up, mocking her words. "There she goes again, Blue. She loves the sound of her own voice, and she wants you to love it too."

"Tell me something that I don't already know."

"You are neither wolf nor dog," Nate shouted from across the floor. He was carrying a bundle of smudge sticks that he lit from a glass Jesus candle that Debbie was holding in front of her. The overpowering whiff of smoke plumed in a white cloud, filling the air with Nate's remembered past.

"It is sacred white sage to protect you," Violet hollered from behind the smoke. As the three of them moved together across the floor, Avaricious started to cough...

Chapter 11

Outside of Toussaint, the Ohio National Guard was called in to reinforce the civilian units that held down the perimeter of the storm. Special Ops troops, arriving up I-75 from the south, soon followed with The Beast, an armor-clad weapon of mass investigation. Built on the same frame and chassis as the Abrams M1A2, the sixty-three tons of military brainwork carried on board four CIA tech soldiers, a secret weapons system with enough Abrams firepower to level a small city, and fifteen hundred horses to move them in a hurry. Equipped with a thermal management system of processors that were linked to the Army's common command and control software, the tech soldiers could immediately transfer digital data and overlays to compatible military systems stationed anywhere in the world. Designed for deepwater fording and operations in any climate and lighting condition, including contaminated environments charged with nuclear, biological, or chemical poisons, it was an extreme instrument of adaptability. Its thermal viewer could see into pitch-black darkness, and its atmospheric sensors could interpret the slightest mutations of air pressure, temperature, humidity, electrostatic discharge, radiant anomalies, and wind. Its tracks stalked the earth on a twelve-foot-wide print that stretched twenty-six feet around perfectly machined, bombproof rollers. It was fast and low to the ground, impervious to the natural elements and any man-made devices short of a direct nuclear hit. Feared by its enemies as the most lethal battle tank weapon in the world, it was the superior choice to probe the interior of the storm, explain the loss of the six Navy drones, and then dissipate the tempest from within.

With all systems prepared to deliver the expected news, The Beast rolled its mighty armor into the fusillade of spiraling wind and blackened sky. Waiting for the upload of scientific data with the greatest amount of confidence, the military network was eager to examine the word, but no word came. The only intelligence that was transferred from the radio interface was the quartet of screams from within the belly of The Beast with the loudest reporting, "Oh my God," and then sharply dissolving into white noise. It would be business as usual outside of Toussaint. The kind of business that men employ when questions go unanswered and fears become easy company.

The Toussaint faithful advanced through the darkness to the sanctuary of the school. There would be no man-kept record of their arrival by hour or by day. Time was a notion that they once lived by; it finally stopped at the here and now. With the tempest consuming all light from the outside world, and their fate bound to their beliefs, time was no longer of the essence. Each step taken up the granite bloodline of the elders was time enough to deliver them to their destination. With sleeping bags and bedrolls, and food to share, and faith to bear them up, the Volunteers came to witness what most outsiders believed would never come; and they were on time.

Coyote stood at the door, shaking hands, slapping backs, welcoming all who entered. It was his regular station during basketball season, where he hawked the fifty-fifty raffle and game ball tickets to home and visiting fans; now, he only served the home team. Dressed in school colors and talking out loud about burning signs, prophesied storms, dead birds, and the path of angels, the Volunteers showed up expecting to win. It was extreme tailgating without the usual elements of grilled burgers and pickup trucks parked neighbor to neighbor three hours before tip-off. Even without the customary game traditions to boost their pride and ignite their passions, they carried with them an unmatched feeling of euphoria, a sentiment above all others when belief waxes material.

Joe stood behind Coyote with his back to the wall and the palms of both hands placed flat against the red Ohio brick. Fired in the giant kilns of the Toussaint Brick Works, each molded block of clay, mortared together to create each wall, symbolized to Joe the strength of Toussaint. Each brick was a testament to what good people could create by working together. Such bits and pieces of life were always an arm's length away from him, waiting to be touched, wanting to be revealed. The brick was much like The Great Wonder in its truthful recollections of life, witnessing what their gatherings produced within the solid walls of the gymnasium. Even though the Volunteers never wondered about bricks and sticks, the clay that such things sprang from was an eye to their world, a record of their existence. From the earth such things were made, and to the earth such things returned, and Joe was satisfied to run between both ends in the period in between. Huddling up with the brick assured him that whatever was coming to their house would arrive in a place where he had the best advantage to protect and serve. He was with his people, and he was no longer vexed by the temperamental tidings of sleep. Joe Water was good to go.

With each greeting that was delivered to him, Joe smiled and called each Volunteer by name. He knew them all, by word and by deed, and he counted heads and asked others to count as well. Nate stood next him, holding the burning white sage with a Shawnee sensibility that still lingered in his understanding of things. It was an honest offering to safeguard what he loved. The strong, aromatic resins produced the protective smoke that was used in the purification rituals of his ancestors. He needed it for a time such as this, a time when he required strength from places where he had never been, a time when he most needed to be himself. Somewhere in the deepness where every man collects his soul, Nate was certain that God would be pleased to be greeted with the naturalness of his intentions. The scent was agreeable, though uncommon to everyone but Nate. It was not the traditional frankincense of the church that he burned during his usual prayer rituals, or even the ketoret that he used when trying to invoke the fragrance of God, but the smell of it flavored the air with such richness of his own legacy that it moved some of the citizens to tears.

The march into the gymnasium continued until the last head was counted and each Volunteer was reckoned for. There was room for everyone, and each family found its place within the sanctuary of the community. When the counting was finished and Joe was certain that every citizen was in the census, he asked Coyote to close the doors, and then he called his entire department together in the jump ball circle in the middle of the hardwood floor. Thanking them one by one, he then released them from their public service. Debbie Marshall then took her place with her first calling, her husband and her four children; her work for the village was now complete. There were no more calls to answer, no more roads to keep open, and no reason to watch the clocks that no longer kept the time. There was nothing left for her to do but wait. She took her family to the top row of bleachers, placed the children between her and her husband, kept her eyes on the door, and then prayed quietly that they were doing the right thing. It was not the kind of prayer that she usually made, but these were not the kind of days that she usually had. For everyone else, between the clamor of praise and the report of approaching blessings, their own quiet prayers were much the same. Following Joe's lead, the fire chief did the same with his crew, and then the mayor did the same with all other public servants. There were no discussions about protocol or historical precedents to follow. Their fate would be met without official title, or responsibility, to act in any way except to stand for each other.

Violet stood next to Avaricious, eyeing her with intentional resolve. If Joe was all right about keeping this creature hovering around the fringes of Toussaint, then Violet was going to keep her within arm's length, a close enough distance to do something if something had to be done. Woman to woman, the power of Avaricious beneath the covering of Joe's coat was still formidable, although Violet was sure that she could hold her own, if given a chance. Violet's thoughts were not held captive by such jealous notions, such mind-numbing vexations of doubt. Those pale imitators would help nobody but the coughing splendor who stood next to her, staring at the floor with bowed head, trying to breathe while the white sage seared her lungs. Knowing all of this, Violet removed a beaded necklace that she had worn faithfully since she was confirmed. A turquoise-inlayed silver cross glimmered from the necklace as she placed it around the smooth-skinned throat of the suffering trickster. The playing field was now level.

Coyote witnessed the merciful exchange and waited for the result. Perhaps the winged beauty would throw off Joe's coat and then vaporize in a puff of smoke, or burst into flames, or melt into the floor, percolating her way back to where he was sure she had come from. He would favor any of these outcomes, but none of them followed. Lifting her head, she looked away from Violet, and then she looked all around the gym as the Volunteers settled in. For the moment, none but a few were interested in her presence. She had nowhere to go and nothing much to do. Surrounded by such indifference was just as challenging as swallowing the talk of God that was blended with the herbal taste of Shawnee smoke. It was a first for the troubled vixen, and with the cross hanging around her neck, she shivered with the thought of it.

As was the custom, when the Volunteers came together in community worship, there were no divisions of church to be recognized, no outside constitution to govern. They founded their fellowship on the fundamental belief that only Volunteers knew what was best for Volunteers regarding their spiritual practices. All were Christians, whether they prayed on their knees or gave thanks while sitting or standing, whether they broke wafers during communion or ate pretzels at Violet's Friendly Tavern before church. They were all on the same page with their impassioned belief that God was real and that he was coming to their house for a final visit. There was also no doubt among any of them, as they prepared to wait, that Joe Water was on his own clock, looking official, solemn, and able to protect and serve. On this occasion of biblical prophecy, they were also certain that Joe would finally speak; but he would not. Instead, with the evangelical boiler needing steam, Pastor Gordon ambled onto the floor. He knew the crowd and had prayed heartily for most of them since they were children. He was the bus driver and the voice of their team prayers since anyone could remember, and if Joe was reluctant to take the microphone, Pastor Gordon had no such uncertainties. With the public address system powered up to peak volume, the gymnasium was now their church, and Pastor Gordon would lead them in prayer.

"The Lord is my light and my salvation, whom shall I fear? The Lord is the stronghold of my life, of whom shall I be afraid?" he proclaimed with rich and confident timbre as he began his delivery of the twenty-seventh psalm.

"Amen," shouted everyone except Avaricious and Joe.

"When evil men advance against me to devour my flesh, when my enemies and my foes attack me, they will stumble and fall," his voice roared.

"Amen," the congregation shouted as though their team had just scored.

"Though an army besieges me, my heart will not fear; though war break out against me, even then I will be confident," he continued, while a glistening bead of sweat traveled down the middle of his forehead and then rolled off the tip of his nose.

"Amen!" they cheered.

"One thing I ask of the Lord, this is what I seek: that I may dwell in the house of the Lord all the days of my life, to gaze upon the beauty of the Lord and to seek him in his temple," he bellowed, wiping his brow with a swipe from his left hand.

"Amen!" they cheered even louder.

"For in the day of trouble, he will keep me safe in his dwelling; he will hide me in the shelter of his tabernacle and set me high upon a rock."

"Yes!" they screamed. "Yes…Yes…Yes!"

"Then my head will be exalted above the enemies who surround me; at his tabernacle will I sacrifice with shouts of joy; I will sing and make music to the Lord!" His voice reverberated as he pointed his right index finger straight up to the heavens.

"Hallelujah! Hallelujah! Hallelujah!" the congregation answered as they rose to their feet, weeping and wailing their approval.

"Hear my voice when I call, O Lord; be merciful to me and answer me!" he pled, pouring the word around the gym and into their thirsty hearts.

"Amen!" they cheered with deafening pitch.

"My heart says of you, seek his face. Your face, Lord, I will seek. Do not hide your face from me; do not turn your servant away in anger. You have been my helper. Do not reject me or forsake me, O God my Savior."

"Amen! Amen! Amen!" Their chorus of voices resonated off of brick and glass, raising the gooseflesh that attends such fevered rapture.

"Though my father and mother forsake me, the Lord will receive me."

"Amen! Amen! Amen!"

"Teach me your way, O Lord; lead me in a straight path because of my oppressors."

"Amen! Amen! Amen! Hallelujah...Amen!" The congregation swayed back and forth in the stands, rocking shoulder to shoulder, heart to heart.

"Do not turn me over to the desire of my foes, for false witnesses rise up against me, breathing out violence." Smelling the win, he paused and bowed his head, and the congregation did the same. Taking a large red workman's handkerchief from his back pocket, he mopped his forehead while deliberately inhaling and then exhaling a loud and drawn-out breath. With flawless timing and stirring flair, he was ready to deliver them to where they wanted to go.

"I am still confident of this"—his voice was near breaking—"I will see the goodness of the Lord in the land of the living. Wait for the Lord. Be strong and take heart and wait for the Lord!" He lifted his head toward the heavens while waving the red handkerchief in the air. Triumph in the word was his, and the Volunteers agreed.

"Amen! Amen! Amen! God is good! Amen!" they thundered in a back-slapping, high-fiving madness that filled them with one collective voice from the glory year. Each man, woman, and child, lathered up in the joy of victory, proudly celebrating the winning team, were carried away in the ecstasy of their beliefs and their history. What a feeling to be part of the joyous pandemonium with the rapture oozing from their pores, but Joe wasn't feeling it. Instead, he stood with his back to the wall, touching the familiar calm of the Ohio brick.

"God is great!" they all shouted victoriously, but Joe was not along for the ride. His attention was on Avaricious and his realization that, standing next to Violet, she looked like a shadow. Violet was alive with a radiant white glow, but Avaricious was a faded kind of dark that had no surface for reflection. Such a gloomy shade of dark could stay hidden even in the brightest light. He looked around and saw Violet's kind of shine emanate in varying intensities from every other person in the gym. Some dazzled and sparkled, while others just glowed, but they all had the light except for Avaricious; from her there was only darkness.

Joe stood several feet away from her, yet even in the deafening roar and wall-rattling cries of jubilation, Avaricious spoke his name and he heard her voice. It was as though the surrounding clamor had been swept away into a vacuum, leaving her words behind as evidence.

"Joseph, you finally see the light, don't you? In this place, only you and I can see it. You are all born with it, but if you step outside of the light, it fades;

remain outside the light, and you can never be more than a dead human."

The crowd continued to chant as she spoke. "God is great! God is great! Hallelujah, God is great!" The dust shook from the steel rafters, but Joe heard only her voice.

"Did you know, Joseph, that you are only light? You are the brightest of all, and they accept it without knowing, believe it without seeing. They recognize you, Joseph, just as I do."

Violet didn't need to see Joe blowing in the wind to identify the sway that Avaricious still had over him. Stepping in front of them to block her coiling influence, she turned to face the dusk-filled being. "Give it up," she said. "Nobody's listening." And then she turned back around, elbowing Avaricious in the ribs.

"I almost had him. Do you want to know how it feels?" Avaricious said, and this time Violet did listen. Spinning on her heels, she went nose to nose with the chattering fox.

"You're a real piece of work. Only God knows what to do with you."

Avaricious did not blink. She spoke calmly, right into Violet's heart. "God does know, and so does Blue Water."

Violet snapped back with a sudden anger. "Shut up, or I'll rip that coat right off of you and show them all what you're up to!"

"Are you sure that you want to do that?"

"Shut up," Violet warned, grabbing her by the arm.

"You just can't let go, can you?"

Violet squeezed her arm with enough force to leave a handprint bruise. "You're nothing," she said before releasing her.

Avaricious brushed her arm where Violet's grip had been. With a stroke suggestive of an unimpressed cat cleaning its fur, she looked away from Violet as she spoke. "We'll see..."

Chapter 12

The first to arrive at Toussaint's gates were the adrenalin-stoked ambulance chasers who raced toward the sound of sirens with quickened hearts. Scattered among this growing crowd were local zealots who came to witness the storm of God. Hour by hour, other pilgrims arrived, curious witnesses to the extraordinary event. State and local law enforcement had little trouble controlling the moods of these gatherers, but when The Beast disappeared, the extreme and unbalanced underground of mankind arrived with cruel and unusual intent. They slipped around the nation's defenses and into the heartland of America, aided and abetted by the mindless few who think that murder is an expression of their faith. In response, a division of Army Airborne troops was deployed with two companies of Air Cavalry, two armored infantry battalions, and a thunderous skyful of fighter jets booming viscous vapor trails that obscured the sunlight. To civilian veterans familiar with military strategy, the troop movements along the I-75 corridor looked like the first stage of mobilizing to a battlefront. Quick-strike ready, their marching orders were to evacuate all nonmilitary personnel, including civilian news crews, to the outside perimeter of a twenty-mile radius from Toussaint. By establishing this field of operations around the flash point, the military had prime advantage; at least, that was the objective.

While arrogant media soothsayers and other diviners of dread were spinning the nation toward a single season of chaos, Toussaint continued to celebrate. Heaving their impassioned bodies in the frenzy of the promised rapture, with sweat-drenched brows and jubilant hearts, they sang and shouted and praised the name of The One they had never seen...The One who was coming soon...The One who would deliver them from whatever they imagined was sitting on the porch, waiting to consume their flesh.

Joe remained calm with his back against the wall, touching the Ohio brick, feeling their love, thankful to have been born in this time with these people. He did not need to see more than what was right in front of him to understand his longing to protect and serve their interests. In spite of their manic behavior, the Volunteers believed in each other as much as they believed in any supernatural deity. The only proof he needed was in the knowledge of the head count. Every citizen was accounted for, and all that it took to get them here was a phone call from a friend. The word did not have to come down from God; a neighbor was good enough. Standing in the blaring harmony of their spiritual confidence was satisfying evidence to Joe that his stretch on the job was time well spent.

The euphoric singing and shouting of praises slowly evolved into a spiritual chanting. "God the Father, God the Father, God the Father" rang out until their voices grew hoarse and their breath short. "God, God, God" replaced the chant with less strain and an easier breathing pattern.

After a length of time that was measured in patience rather than moments, a faint call from one voice shouted out from somewhere in the gym. "Swift-Water, Swift-Water, Swift-Water," the voice repeated above all others until everyone joined in. Soon, the only chant heard was a remembered cheer from a time when all of their expectations were met. "Swift-Water, Swift-Water, Swift-Water" was a call that could be answered.

"Do you hear that, Blue? They're calling our numbers," Nate said, getting close enough to Joe to notice the fresh smell that was rising from his skin.

"Sorry, buddy, this is not a pep rally," Joe answered, still leaning against the wall.

"Sure it is. They want to hear something from their old captains."

"You know better than that," Joe warned, but Nate continued to prod his friend.

"Come on, Blood, it smells like you're ready to talk. What better time than now?"

"Go on, Blue!" Coyote yelled.

"Do it for them, Joe," Violet said, nodding to Joe.

"Swift-Water, Swift-Water, Swift-Water," they continued to chant until Joe felt compelled to do something. He didn't know what, but he had to do something.

"Okay, buddy, but you do the talking," he said to Nate, who turned and then passed off the remaining smudge sticks to Coyote.

As the two of them walked toward the center of the floor, shoulder to shoulder, looking and feeling as though time had never changed them, the crowd went wild. God, they had yet to see, but Joe Water and Nathan Swift preparing to give a pep talk was reason alone to be there. Swooning in the stands, crying out their approval with winded voices, the Volunteers were on a roll that felt like heaven.

Joe was always uneasy about accepting praise, even when it was earned and right to receive. He deeply appreciated their tributes and thanked them with a lifetime of honest work, but he kept most of his words to himself. For him it was enough, at least he gave back, and for as long as he had breath and life to spare, he was committed to continue. This much was second nature to Joe, but blind faith was not; blind faith gave nothing back but an idea. A man is real, easy to be seen and easier to tell if he is good or bad. A good man recognizes what is good to do, and he does it. A bad man turns away from good, doing nothing. Can it be any different for God? It was this enigma of a good and understanding God failing to protect and serve that separated Joe from every other Volunteer, and he felt it most at this moment. As they entered the circle for the last time, he was sure that it never bothered anyone else in the gym, except maybe Avaricious. In this one way, he stood alone on his watch. As Pastor Gordon patted them on their backs and shouted out his last praise to God, another voice spoke only to Joe, and a different hand was laid on his shoulder.

"Joseph, you cannot know the mind of God, but I will let you know how it feels," the stranger said, appearing miraculously beside them in the circle. His voice was clear and familiar, but only Joe could hear it. He spoke with a punishing tone that flushed Joe red with each pronounced word and then gripped his heart and squeezed until he fell down to his knees. The pain was beyond any that he had ever known, beyond any that a man could bear, but it was only the beginning. Attending the wretched pain of his flesh was a staggering anxiety that filled his mind with horrific images of man's worst conditions—those homicidal moments when hand turns against hand for no reasonable purpose; when hungry death meets thirsty death with an agonizing redundancy that is never fulfilled, never satisfied, and reason to kill needs only a crazy man's whim to slaughter the quick and make them dead. The lunacy of it all was inside him, tearing at his soul, sickening him with the gut-wrenching helplessness that he could not stop the carnage. The terrifying affliction was upon him, and it drove him to the floor, into the killing fields of the world.

Nate threw a quick right jab toward the stranger's head, only to have his fist strike an unseen force that blocked his punch with a bombshell jolt to the shoulder. In spite of the throbbing ache, he followed with a haymaking left fist that nearly broke off at the wrist when it slammed against the invisible influence. Pastor Gordon tried his best to subdue the stranger, but was pitched to the ground by a sudden whoosh of air. Coyote dropped the smudge sticks and then sprinted to the middle of the floor, only to be thrown to the ground like the pastor. Violet then charged, and other Volunteers rushed with her, but they were sent skidding through the air until they crashed along the floor in a skinned-up heap. With the celebration turning into a full assault on the repellant energy surrounding Joe, row by row the rest of the Volunteers met the same fate. Nobody could reach him; it was beyond any of them to make a difference. Writhing with the agony of man's misspent existence, Joe's condition could not be put right by those who loved him the most. He was sick with the weight of it and sickened more that he was defenseless before all that he loved.

"How does it feel, Joseph?" the stranger asked, but if Joe had an answer, he couldn't find it among the demented scenes that curled and hissed and coiled within his head. A gagging gasp that rose inside the choking nausea and then gurgled to the back of his throat was all he could muster. He tried to lift himself, to press himself from the floor, but his bones could not support the load of his despair.

"Can you hear their prayers above the crying? Would you answer them if you could?"

Joe rolled over to his back and then spread his arms out; his wrists began to bleed. The Volunteers were powerless to come to his aid. They could not touch him or comfort him or even diagnose the nature of his agony. Somebody shouted that it might be another sign, so Violet shouted even louder for them to join hands.

"Join hands and make a circle around him. Do it! Do it now!" she screamed with authority, and they listened. Joining hands, they tried to make a single circle around Joe, but with more than two thousand banged-up citizens, they had too many bodies in the band with no drum major.

Instead of a circle, they were a hand-holding mob of extras waiting for the next call until Coyote whooped, "Follow me! If Ohio State can write Script Ohio with two hundred twenty-five Buckeyes, then Toussaint can make a circle with two thousand Volunteers." Unlocking hands, Coyote then picked them out of the crowd, one by one, in a marching spiral that started winding around Joe. Advancing around and through each other until every Volunteer was linked together, Coyote managed to lead them into a tightly wound Archimedean spiral with Joe at the pole, Nate and Violet closest to him, and Coyote rotated to be the last man on the outside. It was just a simple problem solved by a man familiar with coiling rope; with a view from the sky, it was much more. Inspired by their creation, in a chorus of shared thought, the Volunteers began to pray.

"Our Father who art in heaven, hallowed be thy name.

Thy kingdom come. Thy will be done in Earth, as it is in heaven.

Give us this day our daily bread.

And forgive us our debts, as we forgive our debtors.

And lead us not into temptation, but deliver us from evil: for thine is the kingdom, and the power, and the glory, forever.

Amen."

As Joe lay suffering on the floor, exhausted and near death, his troubled vision glimpsed a minute point of white light that appeared above the steel rafters. It was a quiet glow of fair radiance that could only be noticed by a man in Joe's position. It was not a flamboyant, penetrating blaze that shimmered beyond a common intensity, commanding one's attention with its brilliance; yet, Joe's weary eyes attended to the light as one holds love when it is first recognized, above all other things, beyond all common reason.

"Are you sickened by their murdering hearts? Are you suffering from their self-destruction?"

A sweetened balm of peace flowed from the light as the words were spoken. As grievous as his blood-letting seemed, his misery found relief as long as he held the light fixed between his brown and blue eye.

Pastor Gordon continued to lead the Volunteers in prayer. Holding tightly to the flesh in hand, they repeated the lines of the Lord's Prayer as a litany, the only petition that they needed. With each repetition of the prayer, their voices simmered into a one-note hum that rolled as resolute as thunder, shaking the space around Joe, but doing little to release him from the stranger. The roar of their supplication was no match for the authority that pinned him to the floor, but it did not diminish their voices, or the sincerity of their convictions, or the red tide of life that was ebbing from Joe's body.

"When do you cuff a man in Toussaint and bring him to his knees? When do you say, 'Enough is enough, I will take no more'?"

The questions being asked were no more than those he had answered every day of his working life. He knew what it meant to keep the peace in Toussaint; his judgment was quick but fair. He knew when to act and when to lay low, and he definitely did not need to feel such searing pain, such manifested guilt and horror, to recognize the difference. This lesson did not belong to him. If it was sent by God, then God did not know Joe Water.

"Be certain, Joseph, time is not with you. You no longer move with the seasons. You flow with your own rhythm that counts not the hour or the day or the consequences of your answered prayers. What you have asked for has been given. What you have witnessed is the result. How does it feel to be God?"

Nate lifted his bowed head from their litany and opened his eyes to see if their prayers were being answered, but they were not—at least, not yet. The stranger still stood over Joe as Joe bled mercilessly at his feet. There was no mistaking the powerfully built, much-talked-about stranger, but who was he?

"Violet, look," Nate said, squeezing her hand, but she did not open her eyes. Immersed in the heartfelt petition of her prayer, she heard nothing but the sound of her own words.

"Violet!" he shouted, compressing her hand with such force that her knuckles popped and snapped.

"Jesus, Nate, you're hurting me!"

"Sorry, Violet, but I was just thinking…What if that's him?"

Hand to hand, one by one the word spread around the spiral until all were listening to Nate's doubt.

"Is that him? I ask any of you. Is that him?"

"Who knows? Nobody has seen him before," Violet answered. "Jesus, Nate, don't you know?"

"I don't know. Ask the pastor."

"Do you know, Pastor Gordon?" Violet asked, but the preacher just raised his eyebrows and continued praying.

"Jesus, Mary, and Joseph, spirits of my tribe, somebody in heaven, please give us a sign," Nate begged, but nothing was delivered.

The Volunteers were stunned. They lived their lives with the expectation that they would know him when he came. He would announce his arrival with signs, and he would show himself in such a way that there would be no doubt among any of them. He was who he was, and there would be no mistaking him for someone else. But now they weren't sure. As Joe's blood continued to spill over the floor, they were vexed by their own confusion. They looked at Joe, they looked at the stranger, and they looked at each other and found nothing but doubt. In the bright light of their moment of glory, they just didn't know...

Avaricious bent down and picked up what remained of the smoldering smudge sticks. Nobody witnessed her movements as she carried them to the door and then threw them into the snow. She could have followed the incense out the door, leaving the Volunteers with their hopeless condition; she could have dropped her coat and flown away. Nobody would have tried to stop her, nobody would even care, but she closed the door instead.

"The dimensions of your thinking are defined by the village limits. Your, days of knowing, have come and gone," the stranger said, and for the first time, they could all hear his voice.

"What does he mean? What is he saying? What, days of knowing? What is he talking about?" The questions rolled around the gym on the wheels of doubt, greased by the uncertain moment.

"What does he mean, Nate? You must know. Joe doesn't hide anything from you," Pastor Gordon said.

"I think we might have the wrong man here," Nate answered, letting go of Violet's hand.

"Bamboozled," the pastor said as everyone in the gym looked on in horror.

"I am Shawnee! I am a warrior! My forefathers were warriors! He who opens the door is with me!" Nate screamed with a remembered ferocity, and then he hurled himself against that which separated him from his fallen brother, raining blow after blow upon the cryptic power within. With savage force he pounded and slashed in a red-faced rage, but the stranger was not dismayed. Standing erect while Nate's furious strikes hit nothing but thin air, he looked around the gym with his infinite stare and then offered his own unblemished hand to Joe.

"It is over, Joseph. Reach for me, and I will show you the way," he said.

"No!" Avaricious screamed. "Can't you see what is happening? Nobody is going to answer your prayers! He is killing Joe! Look at him dying on the floor! Look at the blood!" She rose into the air and then floated over their heads. "What's wrong with all of you? He is dying, and you're just watching," she cried out with such powerful pitch that they covered their ears.

Exhausted, Nate ceased his futile attack. He fell to his knees and then down to all fours, looking to get around what he couldn't get through.

"Is Nate the only man among you?" She rebuked them all as her wings gathered strength beneath Joe's borrowed coat. "You don't know anything," she screamed, throwing the coat off, revealing herself to anyone who had eyes, but she beat her wings with such force that their wide-open eyes narrowed down into watered slits. "You make me sick!" She soared directly above Joe, near the faint light at the top of the ceiling, and then she dove headlong into the impenetrable circle of Joe's despair.

Her flight was so surprising and her delicate landing in the circle so astounding that they only noticed the cut of her wings. Dazed and confused, the Volunteers were bowed beneath the weight of their uncertainty, and the battle that was brewing before them would not ease their load.

"Your pain is but for a moment in the eternal light. Your, days of knowing, is nothing. A thousand years is not much more. Do not reach for him, Joseph; he cannot take away your pain," Avaricious said, standing over Joe's head, dripping with the musky fragrance of her excitement.

"Leave us," the stranger said, still holding his hand out to Joe.

"No more!" she challenged. "Never again will I be an accomplice to your cunning ways. You lured them to this place over their trail of remembered things. You encouraged them with your confident but confusing words, your beautiful but self-possessed appearance. You think that you have them within your grasp, but look, he does not take your hand, and if Nathan could, he would twist it off your arm and throw it to the dogs. This is not going to be a good day for you. You will not keep me from having what is mine."

"You are nothing," the stranger laughed.

"Look again," she said, but he cast his eyes away. "Are you afraid, or are you just shy? Turn your head. You don't matter to me! I am only interested in them. You know their corruptible spirit. It is in their hearts to doubt, to fill their lives with wonder, to think with the genius of their Creator, but then they look away from him when their learning gets too great. Look at them, standing in their own light, and they can't even see it. They are not worth your trouble; leave them to me!"

"You have fallen so hard that your lies sound like common sense. With your flesh as an ally, you think that you have the advantage, but they will know you soon enough, and when they do, you will have no one else to play with," he said, still holding his hand out to Joe without looking at her.

"You have never been human," she shot back.

"And you will never be an angel. Trouble me no more, or I will pull your wings off and cast you into such darkness that you will never find your way out."

"Do it! Reveal your true self. Do not deny them a show."

He raised his head to look at her. "I have not come alone."

She stared seductively into the beauty of his perfect face. "Nor have I."

He folded his hands in front of him. "You cannot tempt me. The light has left the world. These few have kept their light because Joseph's prayer has saved them. You have no light. Nobody is praying for you; nobody will save you."

As the two beings sounded against each other, Joe abided in the light. In a lifetime of keeping the peace, he had never been this close to packing it in, satisfied that his work was done. The more he lingered in the light, the less he thought about everything, the less he felt about anything. The more he bled, the more the Volunteers fell away from their original plans. With Joe helpless, the stranger at odds with Avaricious, and Nate clearly overcome with some venerable warrior spirit, it would take a miracle to set them right. They had not fallen so far that they had forgotten that miracles came by prayer. Even if they weren't sure who would answer, they did what they had always done when all other things seemed hopeless. Pastor Gordon began to pray, and the Volunteers followed, unified in voice, if no longer in their understanding.

"Lord, make me an instrument of your peace.
Where there is hatred…let me sow love.
Where there is injury…pardon.
Where there is doubt…faith.
Where there is despair…hope.
Where there is sadness…joy.
O Divine Master, grant that
I may not so much seek
To be consoled…as to console.
To be understood…as to understand.
To be loved…as to love.
For, it is in giving…that we receive.
It is in pardoning, that we are pardoned.
It is in dying…that we are born to eternal life. Amen."

Needing nothing more than this prayer to satisfy their faith, all of the Volunteers then knelt on the floor to repeat their petition. After the second litany, Nate stood up, and then he sprinted through the doors, making a noise as he left. It was the rustling of meaning, the sound of the wind, the air of purpose blowing through the gym. Nate was not going to let Joe die. It had happened before in their faith, and it was something that he and Joe had talked about at the kitchen table.

Joe said The Old One had given him Tecumseh's words when he passed The Great Wonder into his hands for safekeeping. When Joe studied The Great Wonder, he sometimes thought about these words that the great Shooting Star had spoken to all Indian nations when the foot of Europe fell upon his land.

"When Jesus Christ came upon the earth, you killed him, the son of your own God. You nailed him up! You thought he was dead, but you were mistaken. And only after you thought you killed him did you worship him and start killing those who would not worship him. What kind of a people is this for us to trust?"

Joe called this The Splendid Paradox and testified that it was worth more than a passing thought. After dedicating his life to the ways of Christians, it was time for Nate to stop the talk and continue the fight, in his own way, in his own skin. The Volunteers could stay on their knees, but this absurdity needed a sprinter's legs to pass the stick. Into the dark and twisted night, Nate raced back to reclaim The Great Wonder's power. He had to do something, and this was something to do.

Racing down the granite bloodline, he did not need a light to move through the land that he belonged to; he knew it all, and it welcomed him into the snow. With his arms swinging in perfect memory with his legs, he still ran with the easy flowing motion of his youth. The soft foot strike and sweet speed that defeated all challengers was still with him. There was no one to catch him then, and there would be no one to catch him now. He was what he believed himself to be, running on top of the snow rather than sinking into it, faster than the wind, strong enough to deliver. The seven winged creatures that dogged him from behind had never chased a man of such great faith. God forbid if they ever caught up to him.

Nate could see the red, white, and blue aura of the cruiser's flashing lights in the distant sky. As he entered the village limits, the lights grew sharper, bouncing against the rooftops and through the barren trees, bathing everything in Joe's light, but when he reached Water Street, the sight was spectacular to behold. The lights were shining with such brilliance that any Volunteer would have witnessed it as a sign of God, and Nate was happy to be rewarded.

"Thank you, God!" he shouted as he flowed toward the finish. "Thank you, God!" He gripped the frozen car handle and then pulled the door from its hinges. "Thank you, God!" He reached into the cruiser and grabbed the stick from the backseat. "Thank you, God!" He turned in the middle of the snowy street, where before him parked the seven winged creatures, shoulder to shoulder, looking terrible in every degree of murder. Nate tucked the stick under his arm. "Thank you, Great Spirit! Thank you, Great Creator!" He got up on his toes and ran straight at the beast in the middle.

The creatures let out a deafening roar that sounded throughout every particle of air in Toussaint. Opening their wings to embrace Nate's charge, they driveled with delight over the coming embrace.

Nate's surge was mighty, and his skills were beyond anything that the creatures had ever encountered. Within a breath of making contact, he faked right, he faked left, he faked right, and then he faked left again with such force and quickness that the creatures ended up in a diving pile of snow while Nate swept around their right end. Without breaking stride, he ran with more speed than breath up Water Street, out of the village, past the burning sign, and then back up the granite bloodline to the school.

"Thank you, God!" Thank you, Shooting Star! Thank you, Tenskwatawa!" Full of thanks and renewed hope, he breathlessly charged through the gym door with the stick in his hand.

The Volunteers shouted with surprise when they saw him, a bolt from the blue. It seemed that he had only been gone for a moment; he was faster than they remembered him to be, much faster than he had ever been. Had someone kept a watch on his time, the unbelievable would have waxed material, a miracle to be seen.

Chapter 13

As each man and woman of Toussaint breathed in the inspirational moment, the hours outside the storm quickened with a speed that was relative to the world's ruin. Beyond science and the things that could be explained with zeros and ones, the days of knowing, within the storm equaled years of not knowing without, and in those years, the number of the beast was branded upon humanity, and its number was fear. No summation of the seven deadliest sins could equal the devastation wrought by the product of fear. No mathematician could add metaphor to scripture and arrive at its infinite tally. Its swaggering, insatiable appetite for butchery swelled its belly with each tear shed, with each body claimed, without being satisfied. The prophesied Armageddon rode in on its back, flailing both the good and bad among mankind, stomping their putrefied remains beneath the pathology of their fear. It was never a war of good versus evil, but rather a total annihilation of the dumb and dumber because they were just too afraid to love.

In the beginning, the nation was locked down, the free press was locked out, and the front lines were drawn around Toussaint. The strategy was to restrict public information, thereby limiting the amount of news that agitators could use to stir up public opinion. Most law-abiding citizens agreed with the policy, and for three seasons the general peace was maintained around the flash point. But then, with the crowds growing exponentially and the free press silenced, opportunistic terrorists promoting a proud look and lying tongue sowed discord among brethren of mixed beliefs without being challenged by the truth. Devising wicked plots based on lies, they were swift to agitate the beast, inspiring men who understood nothing but feared everything to shed the blood of the innocent. No one was present to witness and record the first death except those who were responsible for it, and they were not talking. The first killing inspired a witless few to execute three soldiers and then nail their bodies to three ash trees on a shaded knoll overlooking Route Two. A firestorm of reprisals followed, resulting in a murderous clash of beliefs along eleven miles of Lake Erie beachhead. Soon enough, every man was packing iron for protection, and soon enough, every man viewed every other man as a threat. With terrorists of every stripe flowing across the borders, the military response was quick and deadly. In the way of war, collateral damage was the rule. The guilty could not be separated from the innocent. They all fell prey to the bloody claws of fear in the battle for survival. Nobody escaped; everybody was its victim.

The beast unfolded its black wings against the red-lit sky, sowing terror in every man's field, blood on every man's hands. Rising from the sundry wetlands where the milkweed touched the rippled shore and the breast of the earth was ripe and full, where the swamp rose and arrowhead caressed the bulrushes and the succulent round fruit hung sweet and low from tree and vine, the unappeasable fiend flew from this place of dew and then infected the world. There was no antivenin for its fatal bite, no serum for its incurable sting. The winged pandemic feasted and did not rest until little was recognizable in the world outside of Toussaint, or within the mind of Joe Water. As he lay dying on the floor, Joe witnessed it all; it was his gift.

"Help me, oh Great One! Help me, God!" Nate shouted as he hurled The Great Wonder with the passion and conviction that it was the right thing to do.

The stick whistled straight and true to its mark, splitting through that which separated them from Joe, scattering its punitive authority to places unknown. The Volunteers looked on, void of all thoughts but hope, breathing in the wondrous expectation that something good would follow. They watched, they prayed, and when the stick came to rest upon Joe's chest, they expected a miracle, but he did not stir. Violet pushed past the stranger and then kneeled beside Joe's body. She removed the stick from his chest and then handed it to Coyote as Nate kneeled across from her. They watched for more than a half-life of a miracle's existence, but he did not breathe.

"He killed him!" Avaricious said, seeking to gain the advantage from the stranger. She pointed her long, accusatory finger at him, inciting the Volunteers to act. Judging as they, too, would be judged, a rush of red and green zealots swarmed over him, driving him across the floor, pinning him to the wall with little resistance. He did not put up a fight; he did not even make a sound. He just bowed his head and then vanished from their grasp, leaving nothing behind for their empty hands to hold on to.

Nate leaned over the body with both palms pressing into Joe's lifeless chest. Violet placed her hands beneath his head and then tilted it back to accept her breath. Pressing her lips over his open mouth, she trembled, tasting her own salty tears on Joe's bluish skin. With her heart pounding so hard that her breasts pulsed with the noticeable beat, she breathed into him, wishing that he was breathing back into her. Nate watched, waiting for her second breath. When it came, Violet blew more of her life into Joe than he could ever return, but it didn't stop them from trying.

"One, two, three, four, five, six, seven…twenty-nine, thirty…breath…breath." Nate counted while manually pumping Joe's heart. "One, two, three, four, five…twenty-nine, thirty…breath…breath," he commanded as Violet blew more of herself into him. "One, two, three…" The rhythm of their unrelenting hope cried out, but was muffled by the red-and-green letter jackets that silently surrounded them. "One, two, three, four, five, six, seven…" The count continued and would endure for as long as they had breath and life to give—or heaven offered a hand.

"Let me help you," Avaricious said as she stood over them with her full beauty exposed but unexamined.

Nate continued pushing on Joe. Violet gave him another two breaths.

"Please, let me help you." She repeated the offer, but Nate and Violet did not accept.

"Please, forgive me as you have asked to be forgiven. Trust me as you have begged to be trusted, even though you have sinned. Whatever you think of me, let it go. I can help…I know what to do."

Nate looked into Violet's grieving eyes; it was enough. "Do it," he said, and then they made room for her to work.

She moved over Joe like royal water, spreading herself completely over him until his flesh was no longer seen. Immersing the whole of him in the bath of her physical perfection, she laid fallen angel on top of man with all of Toussaint to witness. As they viewed what was before them, the floor began to shake and the walls vibrated with such intensity that the roof split and then opened to the sky. As steel and stones rained down upon them, seven winged creatures flew into the room with a sonic boom that knocked everyone to the floor.

"Listen to my voice, Joseph; we are leaving now. Listen to me…Hear my voice…Come with me," she whispered into his ear.

Joe heard her voice above the crackling static that was in his head; she sounded confident, knowing, and ready to lend a hand. He listened to her as one would heed a remembered sound that brought back the shield of youth, the protective sounds of a safe world where every pain was amended by a father's voice or a mother's song. The melody of her words quieted the hidden battle, obscured the horrors of his apocalyptic vision with the promise of something good, and then lifted him to a place that was both light and peace.

"Look into the light, Joseph; look into the light." She spoke with sanguine assurance.

It was the light that eased his pain from the beating that he was taking on the floor. It was the light that comforted him when fear and hate were all he could feel. It was the light that split the difference between his blue and brown eye before he closed them to the world that he knew; and now he stood before it, outside it, and yet within it, unbounded by space or any clutching hand of man. He was free, and he knew at once that he had died but was not dead, and he was strangely aware that he was without form, and that he was also somewhere, but no place in particular. He had heard of these things, these moments at death when the light beckons and soothes the dying and compels the victim to walk calmly into its dazzling blaze. It was mostly nonsense to Joe until this instant, when in the fullness of his soul or spirit, or at least his thinking, he was somewhere in the light, eyeball to eyeball, and somehow, the light was looking back at him.

Within the soundless moment that stretched before him, Joe waited, but he was not bored by waiting. Self-aware in the same sense that a dreaming man knows that he is not awake, he remained for a time that had no number, no recollection of its length. It could have been one minute, or one day, or one year, or one thousand years; such is the nature of all things when they are in the hands of God. He waited and received only the time before him, a gift that he could not understand; such is the nature of all things when they are in the hands of man.

Joe waited until waiting lost its purpose within the unspoken answer. He waited until somewhere within the slipstream of his waiting, a rustling of light congealed into three solid forms that stood as humans stand, but with no ground beneath them.

"Greetings, Joseph," a familiar voice called to him from the rustling of light that oscillated around the recognizable being in the center.

"Welcome," the other two voices chorused, harmonically on pitch with a soubrette's exuberance.

Although Joe could not see one detail of his own body, he could clearly behold the fullness of those who shaped up before him. It was the stranger, and he had brought company.

"You are one of a kind, Joseph. When others get this far, they always step inside. Nobody ever lingers outside this door longer than an earthly twinkling. They always take the next step; they always embrace the light. That is, unless I send them back," he said as he stood stoutly between two angel-winged companions who glimmered with a golden light.

This was the moment of reckoning, the odd time of stepping in or stepping out of every purpose that he had ever had, and he recognized it in the instant before he found the words to speak; even without form, Joe Water was still himself.

"Where is the one who brought me here? Did you send her back?" Joe asked, finding his voice within the memory of his journey.

"She did not bring you. You brought her. You named her well, and you had her under control until you desired to know the mind of God. She is a cunning and willful essence of every offense that you carried with you, so I turned her away."

"Where did you send her?" Joe demanded, feeling every bit the man that he once was.

"She has gone into the dark hole where she belongs. She has no place with us. That is what I do. I am not much different from you in this way, Joseph. We do not accept lawbreakers and miscreants who have no desire to be forgiven. I only admit those who keep the light," the omnipresent one answered around and through every stretch of Joe's awareness.

"What about the others?"

"There is only you, Joseph."

"What about Nate, and Violet, and Coyote, and the rest of my people; and what about the outsiders?"

"That is why you shine so brightly, Joseph. That is why your light is the measuring stick for all of humanity. It is always the people first with you, even with those who are a challenge to keeping the peace. You wonder about their safety; you wonder if they are still alive."

"It depends on the aggravated circumstance; some are worth a second look."

"There are no more second looks. There is no place to hold them; it is all gone. Every soul on the earth was consumed in the fire of their own fear. You heard their cries when you were in the mind of God, but you ignored their prayers because they were an unbearable thumping in your own broken heart. Even your personal flock, so bright, so promising, was given the choice, and they failed. They could not tell the difference between us when we were standing right in front of them."

"You are cruel. You are nothing like the God that they hoped for. They were only looking to find answers to their questions, and you gave them nothing but confusion. They were good people doing good things, and you turned your back on them with all of your prophetic nonsense. Well I don't get it! You can keep it; it's not worth having!" Joe screamed from within his awakened spirit, but the three beings were not upset. They glimmered, and they glowed, but they did not take offense.

"Our Father? Come on now. Our Father? Where have you been?" Joe continued his fuming challenge. "You are nothing more than an absentee father who failed to support his children. I have never dealt with your kind, but Nate has. He picks them up on the run, and then he locks them up in the county jail with a bail so big that no bondsman will touch them. I have never had such losers in Toussaint. We take care of our own; we do not give up on what we have created. Our Father, where have you been?

Where were you when they needed you most? They didn't fail you; you failed them," Joe rambled on, spilling every bit of himself in an honest wringing of the man. Unlike every other Volunteer in Toussaint, Joe had not expected this day to ever come, but if this was to be his day of judgment, he had a lot to get off his chest. Even without a body to pin his badge to, he was still the chief officer of the peace, and he wanted answers, and he wanted them now.

"Easy, Joseph, you are indeed the quintessential man. You observe the unexplainable and are quick to judge it as God. I have heard it ever since humankind has drawn breath on the earth. Oh, the wind is God, the rain is God, the fire is God, the sun and the moon is God, the universe is God, all things are God; but they are not. It is all so monotonous, so redundant, so lacking in the true original thinking that God has given you. God has created all of these things; they are only an example of the genius of his design. As am I…as are you. I am not God. I am only the Guardian of this place where you are now waiting to reside. I am the gatekeeper of his house, the one who bans the darkness from his mansions, admitting only peace and light. You were born to understand this, Joseph. Where is your sense of duty?"

Joe wasn't about to neglect his obligation to consider the question. He knew the acts of man better than he understood the movements of angels, yet it was plausible that mankind was the egregious party and this flickering spirit was merely a victim. He needed some more details to back up his hunch.

"Do you have any identification?" Joe asked, laughing behind his unseen smile.

"You have a good sense of humor and a better sense of timing, but you're off the clock now, Joseph. There is nobody left for you to cross-examine."

"What is your name? It's always the first question."

"It does not matter what I am called. What matters is that I am recognized when I come calling. I am calling on you, Joseph, and I am asking you to be more than a man, doing a man's job. There is still time for you; you still have time."

"There is no more time. I saw what you wanted me to see, and I felt what you wanted me to feel. What more is there to do but cry, and I don't even have tears for that?" Joe said mournfully.

"It was such a terrible waste, wasn't it, to have so much ability to do the right thing and yet destroy yourself with wrong thinking? That was never the plan."

"What was the plan?"

"His love endowed your kind with such intellect, such curiosity, that you would eventually aspire to be just like him, creating beauty, doing what is right to do, but that's not what happened. Instead, in your arrogance and with your constant fears driving your actions, you tried to be him, judging, but not gifted with his judgment. In the end, Joseph, you were the only one who kept the light. Even though you had doubts, you knew who she was when she battered your will."

"Nate never doubted, and Coyote sure as heck recognized her."

"True, but like Violet, they did not know her well enough when they stepped aside. They believed in her when they feared that their own abilities would not be enough to save you, and that wrong belief was a serious error of judgment. They were consumed by it; they were our last verdict. If those who were so good did not see clearly, then it would not be possible for any of them to see through the darkness."

"Your judgment stinks; your punishment is cruel and unusual. If we were perfect, then heaven would be on Earth."

"That was the plan. He is what he is because he is perfect. You are what you are because you cannot think otherwise. Perhaps I should give you some more time to contemplate the details of your existence. Do you need another hour, maybe a day; how about a millennium? I have eternity to offer you, Joseph, since you are the only one left to consider. How long will it take before you understand the true purpose of your life?"

"I don't want any more time. My people were good, and now they are gone, and my place is with them, not here listening to you. They were filled with love, and respect, and honor, and they were much different than you say. Maybe you don't get it. I'm sure not getting you. I thought that forgiveness was your main deliberation before judgment, not punishment?" Joe was heated by an anger that heaven could feel. Provoked by the light that otherwise soothed him, he appealed the judgment that was handed down to mankind.

The glimmering being at the Guardian's right hand spoke up. "And why is that? Is it because you are only human? Those words have already been given on your behalf, yet nothing has ever changed. 'Forgive them, Father, for they know not what they do.' You can come up with a better defense than this, Joseph. It is old, and it is tiring. They did know, and they just didn't try. But you,

Joseph, you are different, and that's why we're still talking to you."

"I am no different; I am a man."

The shimmering being at his left hand then joined the conversation. "You were a man, a man who was unafraid; that is the difference. That is why you are still able to plead for a reversal in the judgment that has been handed down. Look at yourself, Joseph. Do you see a man? Do you see anything?"

"I see the three of you."

"That is because we make it so; you are only light. Even in your anger you shine brighter than any man," the glimmering being said.

"I like who I am."

"You like who you were, Joseph; you miss it. I know the feeling, but you will get over it. You will understand when you move inside," the shimmering being said as she waved a hole in the light that surrounded them.

"No thanks, girls, and no thanks to you, Gabriel."

"That is not my name," the Guardian answered.

"No thanks, Michael, or Saint Peter, or whatever you call yourself, and no thanks to your two angel buddies. I'm not going anyplace without knowing where I'm heading."

"I am called David Lee," the Guardian said dryly.

"David Lee? What kind of name is that for an angel?"

"David Lee is the name that my mother gave me. Don't be so surprised. We all have a mother, just like you, and these two golden sweethearts also have a name. At my right hand is Anna, and at my left hand is Amber. Don't you recognize them? They are God's seraphs. They made light work of the outcome of snow that you asked for, and then they fought to hell and back to keep you here. The darkness is a powerful foe, but it is no match for the fierce brilliance of God's seraphs."

"My father named me," Joe said, completely embracing his new knowledge. The seraphs were his kind of girls.

"You still have much to learn, but you do have the time to learn it all. God's seraphs will show you the way if you pass through the door."

"What's on the other side?"

"You won't know unless you pass through the door," said Anna.

"You still have a purpose, and an opportunity to fulfill it," said Amber.

"If you fail to act, the world that you could have inherited according to the plan will return to the formless dark of the spreading time," warned the

Guardian. "Any light that was human will dissipate into the vast space from which it arose. All thoughts that once had hope will inherit nothing but the empty range that has no horizon and no point from which to begin or return. Alas, Toussaint, and every parsec of stellar distance that was real or imagined by your people, will be folded into a grain of God's memory. He will be the only one able to recall your likeness; the rest of us will forget you. All that was, will be no more."

Joe listened to every word spoken by the Guardian. He had no one to corroborate information with, so he attended to each word and then weighed them against the veracity of every truth he had known. When he was close to understanding, he asked for clarification.

"Are you saying that there is still hope? Are you saying that if I pass through this door that I can change what has already been finished?"

"You cannot change what has been; you can only affect what is and what is to be. Only God can change what has been," said the Guardian.

"At some point he expected that you would one day be more like him; one day you could join him in this magnificent place that offers a peace that is without equal," said Anna.

"But truth be told, it has never happened because the mystery of him is more than you could ever hold in your head. Humankind can only live on faith because the truth is greater than your ability to imagine it," said Amber.

"You are the blood of the lamb, Joseph, but you are flawed because of your humanity. Even though you are human, you still have the greatest opportunity among men to prepare them for the truth. You cannot change what has already taken place; only God can deliver such things. But you can surely influence what is coming," the Guardian said, looking every bit like a confidential man who was entrusted to hand down the law.

"How can I do this?"

"Spread the news, Joseph."

"What news?"

"God is alive, and he is watching, and he has room for them if they rely on the goodness that each of them was given at birth. God is good! All that he expects from mankind is to also be good, and then only grace and beauty will follow. It is as simple as breathing the air that sustains your human life."

"That's easy for you to say; you're the Guardian."

"It is, Joseph, because with my view from the sky, I can see everything. Tell them to look around at his creation and appreciate what he has made for them. Tell them all to serve as angels in the world of men and to never doubt that he is watching over his work. They will be good by doing good, and their light will shine. As long as they shine, they will have nothing to fear; darkness will not follow them. As long as they shine, I can receive them in his house; there is no other way. It is universal law, Joseph, and the law is something that you have always understood. Everybody who shares the planet must understand that this law cannot be broken by anyone. Spread the news, Joseph, to every man, woman, and child who walks in his garden. Give the message one more time, and give it simply, without the clutter of one million doctrines, and the ornamental icing of metaphor and symbolic glaze. There is no need to be fancy. The message is simple enough. Mankind does not rule the world, but if they want to live beyond it, they must come through me, and they must shine. Goodness is the light; there is no other way through the door."

Joe was somewhere within the formless gleam of the endless light, considering his next move. The Guardian's words were simple enough to understand, plain enough to believe, and Joe was still man enough to find out for himself. He had a definite choice to make that had infinite possibilities, and there was no better time than now to make it.

"I'm ready, girls. You don't have to hold my hand." He hovered between the two seraphs, aware that he was moving, confident that he was going in the right direction.

"You cannot change what has been; you can only affect what is, and what is to be. Only God can change what has been," the Guardian repeated. "Keep it light," he added with a flash of brilliance that would have blinded a seeing man.

Half in, half out of heaven, Joe turned in the doorway to face David Lee. "Thanks, buddy," was all that he said, but it was enough. It was the best that he had to give, coming from the heart that was stirring inside the man. As the door swirled up behind them, Joe was more than he had ever been, and he was ready.

"This is where we leave you," Anna said.

"But it's dark in here. I can't see anything but the two of you."

"It will be light again," Amber said.

The two seraphs rustled their wings, and Joe could feel the air move against him. They dissolved slowly into somewhere, their light reduced to nothing, and Joe was left to waiting once again.

In a time that had no measure, in a room that had no light, Joe heard the rhythm of life in the absolute darkness that surrounded him.

"One, two, three, four, five, six, seven…twenty-eight, twenty-nine…breath…breath."

It was the sound of voices working in the distance.

"One, two, three, four, five…twenty-eight, twenty-nine…breath…breath."

It was a familiar cadence, a beat with determined purpose.

"Breathe, Joe, breathe!"

No one had to agree with what Joe heard next. It was unmistakable, as recognizable as a man's own reflection. It was what he was waiting for, and the sound of it was enough confirmation as to whom it belonged to.

"Can you hear them, Joseph?"

"Yes, God, I can hear them. Where are we? Where are you?"

"We are at the beginning. You are with me, and I am with you." He spoke every dialect of mankind, and Joe understood every word.

"Why can't I see you? Why can't I see myself?"

"You can, Joseph. Look hard within yourself. You can see us both. There is no separating you from me."

"I understand…"

"Then you know that I love you."

"Yes, I know."

"Then you know enough. Your, days of knowing, are upon you. I will change what has been, but you must change what is to be. Are you ready?"

"Yes, I am."

"I love you, son."

"I love you too."

"Let there be light…"

"Clear," Joe heard a familiar voice command, and then a bolt of lightning sparked white across his eyelids as he started to heave the mossy Toussaint wetness from his lungs.

"He's breathing! He's breathing!" Violet cried out, wiping his spray from her face.

"Thank you, God," Nate shouted as he pumped his fist to the sky.

Smeared with the muck and weed of the river bottom, smelling of the storm-imbued ooze that covered his stripped and peeling flesh, Joe was where he wanted to be, and with whom he wanted to be with. The searing pain of his scorched and broken body was no problem for a man who had traveled so far; Joe Water was home.

"Great job, Nate. Good work, Violet," Coyote said, handing a dry towel to Violet. "Now take this light while I get a line into him." He handed the spotlight off to a dark face in the crowd. "Hold the light still," he scolded as he hunted up and down Joe's right arm for an intravenous entry. "He's a real mess, must have been struck by lightnin'. Blue's the only son of a gun who could have stood up to it. Here we go; here's a nice one. You got a good one here, Blue. Hold that light steady now, sweetheart."

"Jeez Louise, Tommy, I've got the light. You sound just like my father. Just make sure that you don't break that needle off in his thick hide," the voice behind the light teased.

"There you go, Blue. Here's a nice dose of somethin' to keep you kickin'," Coyote said as he injected a cocktail of stabilizing drugs into Joe's right bicep. "I didn't even have to tie her off. I remember that vein from back in the day; she was always a dandy. Gather around the gurney now, boys. Take it easy now. You are about to carry a special load of man here; yes, indeed, this is some first-class freight."

The Volunteers massed tightly around Joe, each one wanting a hand in raising him out of his moment of death. "Three on each side is all that we need, just three on each side," Coyote barked as he singled out six men to lift up his friend. The six chosen Volunteers raised Joe gently from the ground, and then Nate, Violet, Coyote, and three other Volunteers took the point and led the way. Steeped in the conditions of the swollen river, they slogged through the storm-battered marshland to the carnival of lights that gamboled upon the bridges.

As they were loading Joe into County Squad Thirteen's wagon, he reached for Nate's hand, and then he started to speak, clearly and with purpose.

"Where is she?"

"What did you say, Blue? You're going to be fine, buddy. Everything's going to be fine."

"Where is she?" Joe repeated through the cleaved opening of his parched lips.

"Who are you talking about, buddy?"

"The woman in the car," Joe said, his swollen face squeezing his eyes shut.

"There was no woman, buddy. I don't like saying this, Blue, but there wasn't even a vehicle in the river. I guess all of these folks came out here just to see you."

"Believe me, Nate, there was a wreck in the water. I tied my lifeline to the wheel. Didn't you follow my lifeline?"

"I followed it, Blue. Feel my clothes; I'm soaked to the bone!"

Joe held tighter to his drenched friend and pulled him closer.

"She was there, I swear it!"

"I've been to the bottom, Blood, and you weren't tied to anything but some timber, something that was tossed into the river by the storm. The river is full of it, and with everything blowing around, maybe you were mistaken?" Nate gently escaped from Joe's grip and then turned his attention to the Volunteers. "Move it! Let's get him into the wagon!"

"Wait!" Joe said loud enough to be heard by all who were listening. "Don't move me until I confirm it for myself."

"You heard the man," Violet said. "His line is still tied up to his cruiser. Just back it up, and we will all see what comes up from the bottom."

"It'll only take a few more minutes, Nate. Joe's stabilized. Who would know better than me? I've never lost a man that I turned over to the squad, and I sure as heck won't lose this one! Just give the word, Nate. I'll do the drivin'," Coyote said.

Joe grabbed Nate's hand once more and squeezed it with surprising force. "Listen to your people. Back it up, brother!"

Nate enclosed Joe's tenderized and bloodstained hand within his own two meaty fists. "Okay, back it up!"

"My pleasure," Coyote yelped, jumping at the opportunity to slide behind Joe's wheel. "I love these big, fast cop cars." He chuckled as he buckled up the seat belt, indulging himself in the pleasure of being in Joe's seat, if just for a moment. He placed the transmission in reverse and then started pulling on the line.

"Heads up, she's comin' up easy, no problem here, piece of cake! I love this cruiser, what a hog! No sweat. Yeah, buddy, this is a man-sized vehicle. You are the man, Blue Water. Yeah, buddy, you are the man...Jesus...Mary, Mother of God..." Coyote shouted as the body of timber broke through the surface. "Open your eyes, Blue! Open your eyes. Jesus, God, look what we have here!" He stopped the cruiser and pushed the emergency brake hard to the floor. Everyone held their breath in the wonder of the moment.

"Open your eyes, Blue," Nate said, tenderly squeezing Joe's hand with the supportive strength of a brother. "Open your eyes, and we will both confirm what we see."

Joe struggled to open his eyes, but his eyelids were burned and fused together by the lightning that had lifted him from the water. He wanted to see for himself the thing that hushed the Volunteers, but he did not have the strength to open what nature had closed. He tried with all of his might to witness the source of their amazement, but he could not; he would just have to take Nate's word for it.

"What is it, buddy? I can't open my eyes. What is it that you see?"

"If you can't see it, then you'll just have to believe it. You will just have to take it from me, Blood," Nate answered with a reassuring grip.

"What is it, Nate? What do you see?"

"It's a cross. It's sticking straight up out of the water. It's a cross as sure as I am standing here telling you. You tied yourself to a cross; that you can believe."

Joe said nothing more. He let go of Nate's hand, and then he smiled as they loaded him into the wagon. His smile was wide and knowing, fitting for a man who had just been raised from the dead.

"That looks like the top of a telephone pole," Violet remarked as they closed the doors behind Joe.

Nate nudged her with his elbow. "For God's sake, Violet, keep the faith, baby, keep the faith."

As County Squad Thirteen pulled away, the Volunteers trailed back to Toussaint and to the house tab at Violet's Friendly Tavern. Such was their custom after a fine and worthy rescue. They had every moment of this night to talk about, and they had all the time in the world in which to do it.

After Coyote lowered the hewn timber back into the river, he returned to the site of Joe's resurrection to retrieve his spotlight, but he could not find it. He searched the area, and he found nothing. He searched his mind, and all he could remember was her voice. She called him Tommy, and she mentioned her father. If there was more to know, it wasn't enough to find his light.

Nate turned the scene over to the Toussaint Police Department and then headed east on Route Two. He was only a few minutes from reaching the hospital when a 166-mile-per-hour blur sped past him in the westbound lane. He hit his trip lights and then quickly turned them off. Picking up his microphone, he radioed the Toledo dispatcher to let them know what was coming. He was off the clock, and he was going to see his friend. Some things were not worth chasing.

Acknowledgment

Thank you to Nate, Joe, Anna, and Amber, who are, without question in my mind, the best people I know. Thank you to Gordon Senerius, who was a light in the darkest moments of my despair. Thank you to Dr. Albert J. Guerraty and the angels of Temple University Hospital, who brought me back from certain death and gave me the inspiration to finish this book.

God bless them all…And God bless you.

Made in the USA
Lexington, KY
29 March 2012